FAMILY THREAT

FAMILY THREAT

Linda Lonsdorf

Library of Congress Control Number:		2010915692
ISBN:	Hardcover	978-1-4568-0068-0
	Softcover	978-1-4568-0067-3
	Ebook	978-1-4568-0069-7

To order additional copies of this book, contact:
Xlibris Corporation
1-888-795-4274
www.Xlibris.com
Orders@Xlibris.com
88605

While this book is meant for entertainment, it also contains some good lessons about life. Don't miss them. Hope you enjoy the book!

Linda Lonsdorf

DEDICATION

To my sweet mother, Waneda White, who sacrificed so much for me and helped shape my character. I love you so much.

In Memory

I dedicate this novel to my father, Russell White, who passed away in 1994 but sacrificed much to send me to college so that I could pursue my teaching career in English and literature, and for my Aunt Doris who shared my dream for this book but died July 1, 2010 before I could complete it.

ACKNOWLEDGEMENTS

I thank retired Captain James Yocum of the Akron Police Department for educating me on police procedures. I also thank Detective Mike Kakoules for teaching me about laws and investigating techniques that were so beneficial as I wrote this novel. Dr. William Kevin Lonsdorf, my wonderful husband, helped me through some of the medical issues in the novel and gave me tremendous support as I followed my dream to write this novel. And I thank my family (Mom, Waneda White, sister, Donna White, and brother, Terry and mother and father-in-law, Clare and Ray Rouse) and many friends (Don Mervine and Diana Kelley) who also lent me their support and critiqued a portion of my novel, inspiring me to continue.

A very special thanks goes also to Tom Secrest, a former high school friend and classmate who designed my book cover, and to Andy Pfaff, another friend who has helped me out for years in my classroom, who took my photo for this book.

CHAPTER 1

SEPTEMBER 6, 6:45 A.M.

Doug, her husband of 24 years, had left yesterday on a short business trip to Chicago, and now that Paul and Taylor were back in college, Cynthia Conrad was getting into a morning routine. This morning, as every morning, she arose early to gather in the daily newspaper from the box at the end of their driveway and then go for a morning jog. After her morning devotions, she would fulfill her daily "to do" list.

With the garage door remote in hand she walked quickly to the door with a myriad of things on her mind. As the door was halfway up, a pair of long legs in black jeans appeared. As the door ascended, a man with ominous features held a serious looking gun and pointed it directly at her head.

"If you want any chance whatsoever, Cindy, of staying alive, you will quietly turn around and get in to the house."

He knew her name, but she didn't know how. The quick glimpse she had of him, she was sure she had never seen him before. Was he here to rob her? What did this man want with her?

Doug owned his own private detective agency, and he had always warned her to never allow herself to be taken to a secondary location. She felt once in the house, she would have one advantage over him. She knew the contour of the house and where everything was. He didn't. She felt his presence right behind her, but then he paused to put the garage door back down again. At that moment, she made her break and ran toward the kitchen. If she could grab the cellular phone, a knife, or preferably make it to a back door and rush out, she had a chance of getting away. Before she could do any of that, he fiercely grabbed her from behind and the struggle began. His arms engulfed her as he lifted her off the ground. She kicked and attempted to bite him, but he had thick black gloves on. Her movements got him off balance and the struggle moved into the great room. A lamp was knocked over as were two crystal candlesticks. She felt she was fighting for her life. He had a black cap on and she managed to pull it off his head. She took both her hands and managed to scratch his face; angered he hit her in the head with such force she went flying into the wall. She was dazed but managed to stay conscious. She didn't see his gun, but if she could manage to make it upstairs to their bedroom, she could grab their Glock out of the side dresser drawer and perhaps scare him off—or shoot him if need be. As he came toward her, she made a run for the upstairs, taking two steps at a time. Her years of jumping hurdles in high school and college were finally paying off.

Quickly pursuing her, she made it to the top of the stairs. He grabbed her ankle and on her way down, she managed to grab a painting off the wall and attempt to hit him with it. His strength was no match for hers, but she got him off balance again. He fell backwards long enough for her to get back up and run to her bedroom for the gun. Just as she pulled the drawer out and reached for the gun, he hit her with such violent force that the phone and lamp on the dresser fell off the table top along with her reading glasses. As she went down her head hit the edge of the table and everything went dark.

It was all playing out as he had planned. He wanted the house to be in somewhat disarray, so it was clear mischief had come to Cindy. The cut over her eye had left considerable blood on the bedroom carpet and on the corner of the table. For such a feminine woman, he was surprised at the struggle she had put up, but he had watched her for quite some time and knew she was the athletic type. He anticipated she would be so afraid at the sight of the gun that she would freeze and cooperate with him. While she was unconscious, he tied her arms and legs, taped her mouth shut and put her in the trunk of her Honda Accord. He also covered her nose with a chloroformed cloth to assure she would be out for awhile longer. He drove about ten miles into a desolate, wooded area where his car was awaiting. He transferred her body to his stolen 2007 Ford Taurus.

Cynthia awakened slowly and realized she was in the trunk of a moving car. She felt nauseas, had a vicious headache, and it seemed like every muscle in her body hurt. Who was this man and where was she being taken? And why was she being targeted? She was obviously constrained—both hands and feet—and her mouth was taped so there was no way to scream for help. She tried to kick out the back lights but her feet met with what felt like steel plates. She sensed she was on back roads, for she never heard other cars passing by or city street noises. He wasn't stopping for traffic lights neither.

One thing was certain. She was in big trouble and doubted whether she was going to come out of this ordeal alive.

CHAPTER 2

Lucille Rogers went to her mailbox when she saw Snuggles, the Conrad's little Shih-tzu wandering the neighborhood. Cynthia would never have allowed that. Imagining that the dog must have accidentally sneaked out of the house, Lucy called Snuggles to her. She came right to her begging for a pat on the head. Lucy was long-time friends with Cynthia and knew her routine. She crossed the street to return Snuggles to the Conrads. As she approached, she walked right into the garage as the door was already up. The car was gone and the door leading into the house was ajar. She took two steps up leading into the house and called out for Cynthia from the doorway. No answer. She poked her head into the house and called again.

"Cynthia, are you home?"

No response, so Lucy, feeling comfortable enough to just walk in, did so.

As she walked through the house, she noticed a lamp tipped over and broken candlesticks. Some papers were strewn on the kitchen floor. A drawer was pulled out. She immediately sensed something was terribly wrong. She quickly toured the main floor, saw a broken picture on the staircase, and called out again. Fear started to well up inside her.

"Cynthia? Are you okay? Where are you?"

She made her way upstairs and saw that only the master bedroom was in disarray—again, another lamp was on the floor along with Cindy's eyeglasses, the phone, and a few items that were most likely sitting on the table. The top drawer was partially opened and she spotted the gun. Then she spotted blood. She rushed to the master bathroom but there was no sign of anyone.

Lucy grabbed Snuggles and ran quickly over to her own house. She grabbed her cell phone and called Cynthia's cell number. No answer. She decided to leave a message.

Her voice quavered. *"Cynthia? Lucy. Where are you? I have Snuggles at my house. She's fine but was wandering around the neighborhood. Your house is wide open and I can't find you anywhere. I'm feeling a little frightened. I'm going to call Doug. Let me hear from you ASAP, okay? Love ya!"*

Fear had definitely gripped her. Something was clearly wrong, but what? What if she were jumping to the wrong conclusion? She had lived in this serene neighborhood for fifteen years and had never known of a crime committed here. Not wanting to incite panic among the neighbors nor to look foolish to police, she thought it best simply to report this to Doug. After all, he was an investigator of crimes. She began to dial Doug's office. Doug's secretary answered. *"Conrad Investigation."*

"This is Lucy Rogers, a neighbor of Doug Conrad's and I need to get hold of him immediately."

"Mr. Conrad is out of the office until Friday. Could one of our agents help you, Ma'm?"

"No, it's urgent that I speak to him now. I believe something may have happened to his wife, Cynthia."

"What do you mean, Mrs. Rogers?"

"Please, I must talk to him. Either give me a number where he can be reached or tell him to call me immediately."

"Mrs. Rogers, why don't you give me a number you can be reached, and I will try to have him call you as soon as I can get hold of him."

"Please hurry! My cell phone number is 330-688-6249."

The secretary repeated the number and once assured it was correct, concluded the conversation in a most professional manner.

Lucy kept looking outside at the Conrads' home for any evidence of movement. Probably in less than five minutes, her phone rang. It was Doug. She told him what she saw, and immediately his reaction was of concern. He had already tried to call Cynthia's cell phone and their land phone. No response to either. As soon as Doug heard about the turned over lamps and the blood, he told Lucy to call the police immediately and get a squad car out there. He would also call his partner to go to the house to investigate.

"Thank you, Lucy. I'm sure there will be some explanation for this and things will be all right, but until we know, there is certainly reason to be concerned."

Doug immediately got on the phone and called his partner, Mitchell Neubauer. They had been partners for nearly sixteen years and best friends since their days at the police academy. He shared the information he had obtained from Lucy, their neighbor and Cynthia's friend.

"The police are on their way, Mitch."

" I'll go to the house immediately, Doug, and check things out. I'll assess the situation and call you as soon as I know something, so stay close to the phone, pal."

Doug called his son, Paul at OSU, not wanting to alarm him.

"Hi, Paul."

"Hi, Dad? What's up?"

" Have you talked to Mom today by any chance?"

"No, I've been working on an English paper this morning. Why?"

"I couldn't get hold of her on her cell or at home and didn't know what her plans were. Just thought maybe you might know."

"Gee, Mom always has her cell phone on. Is there anything wrong, Dad?"

"No, son. just wanted to talk to her about something. I'm in Chicago on a short business trip. Have to bring back some evidence collected for a case I'm working on."

"Okay, Dad. Tell Mom hello for me when you talk to her."

"Ok, son."

Doug immediately dialed his daughter's cell. Taylor was a sophomore at KSU, sharing an apartment with two other girls off campus.

"Hi, Taylor."

"Hi Dad. What are you doing calling so early?"

"Oh, I was actually trying to get hold of Mom but she's not answering her cell or the land phone. Any ideas where she might be this morning?"

"No. I'm on my way to class right now. Anything wrong? Mom's always got her cell phone on her."

"No, nothing is wrong, Taylor. I'll get hold of her soon, I'm sure. Study hard. Make us proud, kiddo!"

"Bye, Dad. Love you."

"Love you too."

Doug dialed Cynthia's cell phone number once again. He heard her cheerful voice message and left a message for her to call him. Fear rose up in him. He was starting to get that very sick feeling inside that many of the families of crime victims described to him when their loved one was missing. This couldn't be happening to him.

CHAPTER 3

Doug decided to call James Pascoe, minister of their non-denominational church and a good friend to both Cynthia and him. Jim had married them and christened Paul and Taylor; they were highly involved in the church and had become great friends with Pastor Pascoe and his wife. For some strange reason, Doug needed to hear his comforting voice and have him pray for Cynthia. Instead of getting the comfort he was seeking, he was shocked by the conversation.

" *Jim, this is Doug Conrad. I'm calling from Chicago.*"

"*Hi, Doug. Is Cynthia with you on your trip?*"

"*No, as a matter of fact, I've not been able to reach her, and I'm a bit concerned. I know she does a lot in the church. You wouldn't happen to know if she's there working on a project, would you?*"

"*Well, as a matter of fact, she was supposed to be attending the Ladies' Bible Study this morning. She didn't show up. I thought it was strange. She never misses. Is something wrong, Doug?*"

"*I'm not sure, Jim, but the police and my partner have been sent to my house to check our home out. I'll keep in touch. Thanks for the information.*"

Doug picked up the phone and called United. "*I need a ticket on the first possible flight to Akron, Ohio. This is an emergency.*"

CHAPTER 4

The Summit County police and Detective Neubauer arrived at the Conrad home simultaneously. Lucy Rogers greeted them and introduced herself as the caller and repeated her story. The police thanked her for her cooperation, asked her to return to her home and continue taking care of Snuggles if she didn't mind, and they would come back to her house for further inquiries.

Sgt. Dennis Parker and Officer Preston knew Mitch Neubauer when they worked together in the police department, and together they walked in the house. Their first observation was that there didn't seem to be a forced entry. Just as Lucy Rogers had described, they clearly saw what looked like a struggle had taken place inside the home. Mitch began taking pictures, not yet knowing if a crime had been committed yet or not, but quite sure something was terribly wrong. Not wanting to contaminate this scene should it be one of crime, they touched nothing. It appeared that at one point there was a hasty attempt to reach a drawer in the kitchen. It was partially opened. Butcher knives were in it, but still neatly aligned in their divided trays, untouched. Did Cynthia try to get to a knife for self defense? Perhaps.

Stepping inside the great room obviously told a story of an altercation—an overturned lamp, crystal candlesticks shattered on the floor—nothing had been uprighted or cleaned up—unlike Cynthia if she had lost her balance and accidentally tripped. There was clearly a small dent in the wall near the staircase in the great room and specks of what appeared to be blood. A painting approximately 18 x 29 had been removed from the wall at the top of the staircase and had possibly been flung down the stairs. Was it an attempt to delay or protect oneself? The frame was broken and the glass covering was cracked. As they ascended the stairs, no other bedroom had seen unusual activity until they entered the master bedroom. Women's glasses were on the floor in the middle of the room and the lamp and phone, which obviously had at one time been on the end table by the bed were on the floor. The top drawer was partially opened and Mitch saw the Glock 26 Doug had bought for Cynthia years ago when he insisted she get her permit to carry a concealed gun. She did so reluctantly. She was such a gentle soul. A fine Christian lady in every sense of the word, but Doug had convinced her that when he traveled on business, he would feel better if she knew how to protect herself and the kids should someone attempt to break in. There was blood on the table corner, significant blood on the beige carpet, and some spatterings on the cream colored bedspread. There was clearly an "*event*" that occurred in this house, and it didn't look good. While no one really suspected Doug Conrad of anything, he was going to have to come home and answer questions, prove an alibi, and the children would have to be questioned as well.

Until Cynthia could be found, it was uncertain if a crime had even been committed, but there was certainly suspicious circumstances. The house was roped off and secured by the two detectives. Forensics was called in to take fingerprints and gather any evidence needed should this turn out to be a criminal case. A BOLO (be on the lookout) was sent out to all police officers for Cynthia Conrad.

Mitch got on the phone and called Doug's cell phone.

"Doug, an incident has occurred in your home. Just what is uncertain. Cynthia is not here, but things look troubling. You need to come home el pronto."

"I'm at the airport waiting for my flight as we speak. I should get in to Cleveland at 2 p.m. Can you pick me up?"

"I'll be there."

Mitch told him what he had seen throughout the house and both agreed that Cynthia would not have left the house in such a mess nor would she leave the house unlocked or the door ajar. There was clearly a trail of menacing behavior. Hospital emergency rooms had already been called with inquiries to Cynthia Conrad with no results. Meanwhile, a search was on for the Honda Accord. Finding the Honda could lead to the answers they were seeking.

Doug sat on the plane, leaving unfinished business in Chicago. That would have to wait for awhile. Hopefully, his client would understand. This was an emergency, but he hoped it wouldn't be life changing for him or his children. As fear overwhelmed him, he prayed and then reviewed what his first steps would be when he arrived home. He knew the routine questions the police would ask of him and his children. The sooner they could allay their suspicions about their being suspects, the quicker this case could proceed. It was time to tell Paul to come home. Upon arriving in Cleveland, he would tell Taylor to come home, but for now, he didn't want his kids to become hysterical or to think the worst.

He and Cindy had been married for nearly twenty-five years. In fact, their anniversary was coming up soon and they had planned on going on a cruise. They had met in college and had become close friends. She had thick, brunette hair, green eyes, and the most perfect complexion and teeth. Her laughter was contagious, and she was the most goal oriented person he had ever met. They shared a few classes together but he had been smitten by her from the time he met her. She needed a little convincing for awhile, but their mutual respect for each other led to a warm and loving marriage and comfortable life together. She volunteered at their church in so many areas—whether it was rounding up clothes for the missionary barrel, singing in the choir, teaching Sunday school, being involved in church camp and other youth programs, or helping in grief counseling. She volunteered at Akron Children's Hospital assisting in social events that brought in money for services to help the children; she was a regular for serving in the soup kitchen at Haven of Rest for the homeless. There was not a more compassionate soul than Cynthia Conrad. She loved her church, her pastor, and her God. She loved her family. She was the perfect mother for their two kids, chauffeuring them to school activities, being the room mother during their elementary years. She was a Girl Scout leader for nearly ten years, and set a great example for her children and any one who knew her. No one in his right mind who knew her would want to hurt her. Surely, there has to be some explanation for this.

Doug was trying not to let his thoughts carry him to places he feared to go. After all, Cynthia was a strong, healthy woman who used common sense and didn't panic easily. Oh Cindy, when we find you—and we will find you—I will buy you twenty dozen red roses and ten pounds of chocolate. Just please be alive.

CHAPTER 5

Mitch picked Doug up at the airport and arranged to take him home first so he could see the house and talk with Sgt. Parker who was assigned to the case—if there even was a case. He would then be required to go to the station and be interviewed. Doug knew the routine and anticipated the questions he would be asked. The sooner he could allay their suspicions about him, the sooner this case could move along—if Cynthia hadn't shown up by then. As soon as Doug walked into the house, he met Sgt. Parker and Officer Preston who were awaiting his arrival. While he walked from room to room, his experience told him that something bad had befallen Cynthia and his hope was fading that this would have an innocent conclusion. This theory as to how things played out in the house were the same as Mitch's and the two officers who had taken pictures and filled out a report. An alert was placed to find the Honda Accord as well. It would be just a matter of time in finding the car. Fingerprints had been taken throughout the house and were being cross checked. Doug tried calling Cynthia on her cell phone once again. He heard the ring coming from the kitchen. There on the kitchen counter somewhat obstructed by a pile of recipe cards was Cindy's cell phone. Thus the reason why she hadn't been answering it. Mitch bagged the phone for evidence to give to Sgt. Parker.

Fear had been written all over Doug's face, and Mitch, knowing what a great marriage Doug had, sensed the emptiness and fear Doug must be experiencing. Trying to process it all, Doug said, *"Mitch, it's clear something bad has happened in our house. No forced entry, but it's so unlikely Cindy would have opened the door to a stranger, so who was here and under what pretense? Why would anyone want to hurt Cynthia? She was so good. Was this a random act? Could it be retaliation for something I may have done?"*

After all, his life's work was to help convict people of crimes they had committed and to put them in prison. He was the one who had many enemies. Mitch did his best to comfort his best friend, but it was a poignant moment.

"We're going to find Cindy and solve this problem soon, Doug. You're too close to the situation, so you've got to sit back and let the police and your team of buddies work this case."

Just then Taylor pulled in to the driveway in her 2005 Honda Civic. Doug and Mitch met her at the door. She looked troubled.

"Dad, what's going on? Where's Mom?"

Doug put his arms around her and held on for what seemed like minutes. Before he walked her into the house, he began to warn her about what she would be seeing and admonished her not to touch anything just now. As soon as she saw the broken candlesticks and the lamp on the floor, she began to sob, but it wasn't until they stepped into the master bedroom that Taylor became hysterical. The sight of her Mom's blood overwhelmed her. She couldn't be comforted.

"Dad? I'm home." Paul had arrived. *"Oh, my God, what has happened?"* *"Don't touch anything, son. We're coming down."*

Paul was pallid as he looked around the great room—upturned lamp and candlesticks, the knife drawer half pulled out, and saw the broken picture on the staircase. Doug's arms enfolded both Paul and Taylor as they stood in the room weeping. Doug and Mitch promised they would work 24/7 to find Mom and bring her home safely.

"Your Mom is a strong and capable woman. She'll use her survivor skills to stay alive. For now, all of us need to meet Sgt. Parker and Officer Preston at the police station and answer routine questions as

we are all suspects at the present time. They will ask about when we last saw your Mom, time frames, our relationship with her, etc. Just answer honestly."

Mitch drove all three of them down to the Summit County Police Department. All three were taken into separate rooms and interviewed.

"Doug, you know I have to ask you these questions—that it's normal procedure, so don't take offense to this. We have no doubts that your alibi can be confirmed and that your family had nothing to do with whatever may have happened to Cindy."

"I understand. Let's get started."

"How long have you and Cindy been married?"

"It will be 25 years February 14th."

"Were the two of you having any problems in the relationship?"

"None whatsoever."

"Are you having an affair?"

"No."

"Have you ever had an affair while married to Cindy?"

"No. I have always been monogamous and faithful to her."

"Was she having an affair that you knew of?"

"No. We have both a terrific marriage and family and would never do anything to jeopardize either."

"Do you know anyone who might want to hurt her?"

"No."

"Anyone who was angry with her?"

"No."

"Any problems between Cindy and either Paul or Taylor?"

"No."

"Has anyone threatened her life or yours recently or in the past that you can think of?"

"No."

"Anyone who might dislike either of your kids and want to hurt Cindy to even a score?"

"No, not that I know of."

"Are there any of your neighbors who don't get along with you or your family who might cross the line and bring harm to you?"

"None that I know of. We have a good neighborhood and great neighbors." "Are you working on any cases where your life or the safety of your home has been threatened?

"No, but that doesn't mean I would know about it. That's always a possibility in our line of work."

"When did you last see your wife, Doug?"

"Yesterday afternoon. She dropped me off at the airport at 4 p.m. We kissed goodbye. I called her at 10:30 p.m. to say goodnight and let her know I arrived in Chicago safely and was in the hotel. That was our routine when I was away on a business trip."

"What was the nature of this trip, Doug?"

"I needed to check out an alibi of Mayor Stanwick's nephew in the double homicide of old Mrs. McGrary and her caretaker, Madeline Stover, and look for the gun believed to be the weapon used. Allen Stanwick is a person of interest in the murders, as you know, and I was hired by Mrs. McCrary's only niece to find evidence that would point to the perpetrator. Mayor Stanwick is sure his nephew will be exonerated once the weapon is found, so he actually financed my trip to Chicago to expedite the investigation."

"And did you find the weapon?"

"I was working on that when my office called me and told me Lucy Rogers, our neighbor and a great friend to Cindy, needed to talk to me. That's when I found out something might be terribly wrong at home."

The questions continued until Sgt. Parker was convinced he hadn't left a rock unturned and could eliminate Doug Conrad from being a prime suspect. Both Taylor and Paul were in separate interrogation rooms undergoing the same kind of interrogation. When it was finally determined that neither teen held a grudge against the mother, were at their perspective colleges—in class—and had clear alibis, the case could now move in the right direction. He had closely observed Doug's reactions as he walked through his house earlier and had seen the emotionally torn look on his face at the discoveries. This was an impeccable family. Doug Conrad was a lucky and enviable man. But perhaps his luck had run out.

CHAPTER 6

The car ride had become exceedingly bumpy and Cynthia knew they had been riding on rough terrain—probably on a dirt road or perhaps even in a field. She felt terribly weak and groggy and knew she had been drugged in some way. Restrained, there was no chance for escape. Would he kill her as soon as he got her out of the trunk?

Would her life end here and now? No time for goodbyes, no motive? Would her death have no purpose? Could she talk this person into letting her go? She was a persuasive speaker after all. She had common sense, was usually non-judgmental, and perhaps could reason with this man. She had no time to think about strategy. Just then the car stopped and the driver's car door slammed shut. She heard him walking away and wasn't sure if this was good or bad. She would surely suffocate in this car. Cries for help would go unheard if indeed she was in a remote area, and she was almost certain of that. On the other hand, if he opened the trunk door, there was no surety he wasn't going to kill her right then and there. The way he hit her while in the house told her he was not a person to be reckoned with nor did he care about her personal safety. Make no mistake. She was in danger. Terrible danger.

CHAPTER 7

She heard the key in the lock and the trunk lid was lifted. Helpless as she was, he picked her up and threw her over his shoulder as if she were weightless and carried her through a wooded area until they came to a clearing. She tried to look around so she could assess where she might be and if there could possibly be a mechanism for escape. He took a step up carrying her through an open door to what appeared to be a shed of some sort. Certainly, it wasn't a home with a bathroom, running water, and creature comforts. He basically dropped her on the floor in the corner, and excruciating pain in her left shoulder went down her arm like an electrical shock. The door had been left open and daylight made its way into the very small area. She got a good look at him. She would prepare a police description of this man in her memory should she need it. However, she wasn't stupid. If he lets me get such a good look at his face, it is only because he knows I will not live long enough to reveal his identity to anyone. Something just wasn't right with this guy. He was either stupid or he was smart like a fox. One thing was certain. He had a clear plan, and she thought the time was coming that she would soon know what it was.

CHAPTER 8

T he man left the door slightly cracked so that some sunlight could enter. He didn't seem to worry that anyone would be wandering nearby. He looked to be about six feet four, perhaps 240 lbs., very muscular, dark brown hair with a very receding hairline.

He hadn't shaved for several days, it appeared, and he seemed to be "in control" of everything he did. There was no fear or uncertainty in his face that she could read. He bent down to her and tore the duct tape off her mouth. It hurt, but she was glad it was off.

"You scream, you die. Got it, Cindy?"

"Yes," she said. *"I like to be called Cynthia. How do you know me?"*

"I don't. Let's just say I know your husband. I have a score to settle with him."

She wasn't sure if this could mean a compromise or that a deal could be worked out with him. Maybe she had a chance of surviving this after all. With Doug gone and the kids at school, it might take until Doug called tonight or even got back from his trip to realize she was actually missing. The trail could be cold by then, but she had faith in her husband's detective work and that of the police. She felt a glimmer of hope.

"My husband is a good man. If he's wronged you in some way, I'm sure he would try to make it right if you give him a chance."

"Lady, there is no way he could make it up to me! He sent me away to prison for fifteen years. They were long years. My wife divorced me immediately and I lost my sons along with her. Not one of 'em visited me while I was in prison. They want nothin' to do with me now except one of 'em."

"I'm sorry." Appease him, Cindy. Earn his trust and empathize with him.

"The entire time I was in prison, I vowed to go after him and take away everything that matters to him, so he could know how it feels."

"I tell my children the heaviest thing a person can carry is a grudge."

"Well, lady, my burden will soon be lifted."

"You can pick up the pieces of your life. It's never too late to become what you might have been."

"Hell, yes, it is, but vengeance will be sweet."

"What do you plan to do?" Cynthia asked.

With a smirk on his face he replied, *"I'm going to kill you and then kill Paul and Taylor."* Cynthia cried out when he spoke the names of her children. He seemed to know all about them. If he could get her, he could get the children just as easily.

"I want Dougie to suffer slowly, wondering where you are, who has you, and what's happening. And then when he gets so preoccupied over your disappearance, he will find Taylor and Paul missing. But, then, I want him to have the pleasure of finding you all dead. Only then will he know what it feels like to lose everything that matters in life."

Cynthia now knew he was not a reasonable man, that he was filled with hatred and bitterness, and she probably would not be able to talk him out of this plan. Her hopes were dashed and so the reign of terror continued. If she didn't escape, there would be no hope.

CHAPTER 9

SEPTEMBER 7

Sgt. Parker got a tip that a car resembling the description of Cynthia Conrad was spotted off Rt. 224, in a wooded area close to the Berlin Reservoir. The caller provided a license plate number that matched that of Cynthia's Honda Accord. Sgt. Parker and Officer Preston drove out immediately and confirmed it was indeed Mrs. Conrad's car. With latex gloves, Officer Preston pushed the trunk button and the lid popped open. With a sense of fear of what they might find, they lifted the lid. No body. That offered hope, but they definitely found stains on the trunk floor that could not be mistaken for anything but blood. The investigative team was called to take photographs and do some tire track testing prior to having the car impounded. They canvassed the entire area searching for any signs of movement or for a body. This scenario had played out all too often under Sgt. Parker's watch, but when it is the wife of one of your own, it becomes very personal. Doug Conrad had worked on the police force for over ten years before he decided to own his own investigation service. There was not a finer man than Doug. With reluctance Sgt. Parker called Doug on his cell phone and informed him that their car had been found with some blood—though not significant amounts of blood—on the trunk floor. Doug insisted on going to the scene to look at the car, but was quickly denied. Dennis Parker once again called the forensic team to the scene to run tests and take pictures before the car was impounded.

"Doug, I think we need to sit down with your kids and agree upon a strategy for handling this case. Perhaps the time has come to get in front of the cameras and make a plea."

Doug hung up the phone with Sgt. Parker and informed his children that the car had been found undamaged but some blood found in the trunk.

"She's dead, isn't she Dad?" asked Taylor. Tears were streaming down her face. Paul put his arms around his sister as did Doug.

"I'm going to be honest with you kids throughout this ordeal. No matter how it ends, we are going to hold out hope until the very end. Right now, it doesn't look good, but because there was no body in the trunk and not much blood, we can deduct that she's probably been taken to a secondary location."

"Well, if she was kidnapped, why haven't we heard about a ransom, Dad?" asked Paul.

"Maybe we will, Paul. Perhaps this person wants us to sweat for awhile so we are ready to accept his demands."

"What are the police doing to help find Mom, Dad?" Taylor asked in a frustrating tone.

"Perhaps forensics will pick up fingerprints, hairs, etc. that can be traced. The blood will be tested to see if it matches Mom's or belongs to someone else. Sgt. Parker suggested we make a plea on television and maybe draw someone out who knows something. We're going to meet with him to discuss when we should do that and what we should say."

CHAPTER 10

Jim Pascoe dropped by the house to check on the Conrads. Paul had been such a great help to the church. He mowed the church's lawn for the past five years and never charged the church a cent. He had been active in helping out at church camp for the younger children and Taylor worked in Bible School and in the kitchen at church camp for a number of years. Great kids. Cynthia was an amazing woman, and it was hard for him to fathom that something violent may have happened to her. She had worked vigorously to build up a supply of clothes and food for the missionary barrel, she sang in the choir. She taught Sunday school and was active in the Women's Bible Study every Wednesday morning. The church would feel her absence in a mighty way, and it would certainly tear up one of the nicest families in the congregation if something menacing did happen to Cynthia.

When Pastor Pascoe stepped inside the Conrad home, he was warmly greeted by Doug, Paul, and Taylor. He could feel the emotional strain felt by all three of them. He had been in their beautiful home numerous times. It had always been filled with laughter and joy, but today there was none. The somber mood seemed to permeate every room. Doug apprised him of some of the facts of the case—as much as he was permitted to reveal so as not to jeopardize the case. Pastor Pascoe volunteered to bring food in from the parishioners and to help them in any way he could. Our church family will be there for you. As they sat in the living room, Pastor Pascoe led in the most heart-warming prayer, and it did bring hope and comfort to the family. He was such a kind-hearted man, and they appreciated his visit and concern so much. He promised to keep in touch, and they knew he would. He was the truest of friends to their family.

CHAPTER 11

"*I* need to go to the bathroom."

He bent over and took off her shoes.

"*Why are you doing that?*" she asked, half knowing the reason.

"*If you try to run, you won't get far in your stocking feet. Not in this terrain anyways.*"

He pulled her up by her left arm in a rough manner. She didn't think her arm was broken, but it could be out of the socket. He untied the rope around her feet but kept her arms tied behind her. He led her into the woods about fifteen feet away from the shed.

"*Please, I can't do this with my arms tied behind me. Could you untie me. I promise I won't run.*"

He walked over to her, leaned her against a large tree and pulled both her sweat pants and her panties down.

"*Step out of these,*" he demanded. "*Please, please...*" she whimpered. She felt she had no other choice but to surrender, so she did.

"*You're goin' to have to rough it, Cindy. Somethin' you don't look like you're used to. In prison, you can't take a leak or a crap without someone watching you. There's no privacy. Step behind the tree and do the best you can, but if you run, you will be dead by the time you take three steps. Do you understand?*"

"*Yes. Is there some toilet paper?*"

"Get real, lady. Look around. Do you see any?" She quickly voided.

He watched her the entire time. She tried looking around for a trail or means of escape. There was none visible. Thick foliage. Her arms were falling asleep from being in the same position for so long. He stepped toward her and assisted her in putting on her sweats.

"Where are my panties?"

"My prize, Cindy. I have big plans for your panties. Thought maybe Doug would like to have 'em—a final souvenir from you."

Tears streamed down her face as she thought about the emotions that would go through Doug when he got them—if indeed the guy was telling her the truth. Her insecurity increased. If he was to be believed, her days—or hours on this earth— were limited. He returned her to the shed, tied her feet again and left, locking the shed. She heard the car start up and realized she was being left alone for awhile. That would give her time to try to free herself and find a way to escape from this shed. It seemed impossible, but surely there was a way. This would probably be her only chance, and she had to take it.

CHAPTER 12

SEPTEMBER 8

A package was delivered to Doug Conrad's office—a special delivery with CONFIDENTIAL written in all caps above his name. Doug's secretary took the package to Mitch. There was no return address on this package. Mitch was somewhat suspicious of this, not knowing if it might be related to Cynthia or not. He called Sgt. Parker first who then asked Mitch to take it to the Conrad home and together they would watch Doug open it. When they were all gathered, Doug opened the package and found Cynthia's panties. There was a note:

"You caused me to lose my family. Now you'll lose yours. By the way, Cindy was beautiful. Thought you might want these for sentimental reasons."

They were definitely Cindy's panties. The kids had gone to the store to pick up some items at the grocery store. Doug was grateful the kids weren't here for this discovery or it would have been too overwhelming for them. It was more than he could bear. Doug tried not to let panic overwhelm him as he tried to assess what the note meant. So this was happening because of him. Who might he have caused to lose his family? Was Cindy dead? He never came right out and said it, but he referred to her in the past tense. If I'm going to lose my family, does that mean he is threatening my kids and myself as well? Doug had been responsible for providing evidence that sent many a criminal to prison. Was there any case that stood out, however, where a parolee would seek such revenge? Probably many. Why now? Is it possible that this person was just recently released from prison? It would take endless hours of research to find these people, but it could be done. After he processed all of these possibilities, Doug focused on Cynthia and what the panties seemed to imply.

"Dear God, no, no, no. Help me save her, dear God. Help me find her and save her."

Every emotion he had carried deep inside him for the last two days gushed out.

CHAPTER 13

It was clear to everyone what needed to be done next, but Sgt. Parker verbalized it.

"Your home needs to be secured, Doug, and your children need to remain in the house at all times until this is all over. It would seem that your kids may be the next targets. They cannot return to school under any conditions right now as they would be too vulnerable."

Doug, of course, agreed.

"I will place an officer on duty 24/7 to sit in a car right outside your house, and do a surveillance every 30 minutes," continued Sgt. Parker. *"Meanwhile, let's get your family on the evening news in hopes this dude is watching and can draw him out or force him to make more mistakes. Call your kids right now, Doug, and tell them to get home quickly and to be vigilant. We will have the panties and the mailing package tested for fingerprints and DNA in hopes this dude has made his first two serious mistakes. No one should know about this package—not even the press—and I think it best, Doug, that you not tell your kids just yet. Since he didn't ask for a ransom, it is likely he wants to inflict pain upon you, and that would be through hurting your family members. This guy is really scary, Doug."* Doug couldn't have agreed more.

"Mitch, as soon as the kids get home and security arrives, we need to get to the office and go through our files. We need all of our employees

working on this to find who has recently been paroled that I helped send away."

"*I am going to get Channel 5 out here within the hour to break this story and have you and the kids ask for Cindy's safe return. The more people on the lookout for Cindy,* the better. *As you well know, sometimes this works, and sometimes it doesn't, but it's worth a shot!*" responded Sgt. Parker.

CHAPTER 14

Taylor and Paul walked in to find their Dad with Mitch, Sgt. Parker, and Officer Preston. They put the groceries down on the kitchen counter.

"What's up? Something happen while we were gone?"

Doug answered the concerned looks on their faces.

" We need to prepare for tonight's televised news on Channel 5. We need to ask for your Mom's safe and quick return to us. Maybe, the perpetrator will have sympathy on you kids. Perhaps your Mom will be able to see us on TV and know we're desperately searching for her. It will give her hope and comfort. Meanwhile, Sgt. Parker has reason to believe you both may be in harm's way. He wants you confined to the house until otherwise instructed and keep our security system on at all times. Do you understand?"

"Yes, Dad, but what about school? We're going to get way behind."

" Use your cell phones only, and call the school and talk to your instructors. Explain our situation and retrieve your assignments. I'm sorry, for all of this, but we're in this together. I promise you, we won't give up until we find your mother."

"We know, Dad," they both said simultaneously. *" Mom's more important than school anyway. Besides, I doubt that we can even stay focused on our studies until Mom gets back,"* said Taylor, trying to stifle her tears and panic.

"I know, Taylor. I know."

"Dad," asked Paul, *"do you think the guy who has Mom will try to call our home?"*

"Probably not; it would be too risky on his part. The call could be traced and he couldn't take the chance of getting caught."

Paul was getting a bad feeling about this whole thing. Something seemed fishy about these new rules. For sure, things weren't falling in place like on TV.

CHAPTER 15

Cameras and lighting were being set while Sgt. Parker and the reporter for Channel 5 were coaching Paul and Taylor about what to say while on the air. Sincerity and sympathy needed to be portrayed. That would be easy for them. Hopefully, it would draw someone out who knew or saw something that could help break this case and bring their mom home safely. When the public sees how devastated this family is, surely someone will come forward, especially when given the opportunity to remain anonymous.

"5,4,3,2,1 . . . Action." "Last Wednesday morning on Sept 6th, Cynthia Conrad, a 42 yr. old mother of two college students disappeared from her home, but what has happened to Cynthia Conrad and why remains a mystery. There was enough evidence, however, to lead authorities to believe that foul play has occurred but the police won't reveal just yet what led to that theory. Her husband, Douglas, who owns his own investigation firm and the two children have been eliminated as suspects. I'm here at the Conrad residence now speaking with Cynthia Conrad's husband, Doug, and their two children.

"So what do you think has happened to your Mom?"

"We have no idea, but we believe someone took her against her will. My mother would not leave without telling us where she was going. We talk to her everyday, so this is very unnatural. We just want her back," said Paul earnestly.

Taylor added tearfully, *"Please, if you have our mother, let her go unharmed. We love and need her so much!"*

Doug had his arm around his daughter and chimed in, *"We won't ask any questions. If you know where Cynthia is or who has her, please come forward. We love her and need her back home with us. If you have her, we beg for her safety and ask you to contact us."*

"The Akron police are asking anyone with any information about Cynthia Conrad's whereabouts to contact them at 330-735-4400 right away. I'm Linda McCullough with Channel 5 News."

Once all of the news people and their staff left, the police reminded Doug that his telephone line was being traced so if he, rather than the police, received a call of interest as a result of this newscast, he should have the operator trace the call within three minutes. A policeman on duty was sitting in his police vehicle in front of the Conrad home keeping watch of their home and the surroundings. Everything that could be done, was being done.

CHAPTER 16

As Doug, Paul, and Taylor sat around the kitchen table eating food brought in by the neighbors and their church friends, they discussed the telecast—how it went, what they each hope will happen as a result of that, and how long it will take for someone to step forward. While Doug stayed upbeat in appearance for the sake of his children, he knew more of the facts than they. It was *what* he knew that made his hope dubious. Doug discussed who should answer the phone if it should ring and presented several scenarios. He made it clear that their lives, too, could be in danger until they know who has Cynthia and why. He stressed the importance of being vigilant even while in the house. Drapes had been pulled, and Paul and Taylor were told to stay away from the windows. Their lives would not be normal for awhile, but they were to strive to work together as a family and keep up with any college work that they possibly could. Mom would want that. Both kids agreed. Doug was so proud of both kids. They had never given Cynthia or him any trouble whatsoever while growing up. They were normal kids who made mistakes like any other, but they were warm, kind, polite kids who were family oriented. The evening pressed on until there was nothing more to say or do to bring their mom home, so they went to their perspective rooms for the night.

Doug stepped into their walk-in closet and glanced through Cindy's clothes. He got a waft of her Chanel #5 cologne on one of her blouses.

It was as though she were in the closet. He could feel her presence. He studied all of her bright colored clothes and remembered how stunning she looked in each one of them. Would he ever see her in them again? It was more than he could endure. He slid the sliding glass door open and stepped out onto his balcony. Three days had passed and the trail seemed cold already.

He tried to rerun everything in his mind again. Cindy would have put up a tremendous struggle if she could have. She knew to fight, and from the appearance of the house, it was obvious a struggle had ensued. Cindy must have been taken down rather quickly and been taken by surprise. But how? There was no forced entry. Was it someone she knew? But if so, who? The note implies it is someone I ticked off through my work. But, again, Cindy wouldn't have allowed a stranger into the house. She knew better than to open the door to strangers. She wouldn't, would she?

Hope had remained in his heart until the package had been delivered. The note. Referring to Cynthia in the past tense. Insinuating that other family members were in danger. Should he have told his kids about the package? Could they handle that right now? He didn't think so. He didn't want them panicking nor becoming hysterical. He needed them to stay focused and stay aware.

As he looked out at the wooded area behind their house, the moonlight shone through, casting shadows everywhere. He never felt so alone and deserted and hopeless.

How could he stay strong for his kids when he himself was falling apart inside? The love of his life was missing, maybe even gone forever. Not knowing was terrifying. It was 10:35 p.m. and though late, he called Jim Pascoe. Pastor Pascoe answered on the second ring before Doug had time to have second thoughts about hanging up.

"Jim? This is Doug. I . . . I can't see the sun coming up tomorrow. Without Cynthia, I don't know if I can go on . . . I'm so afraid. I feel so alone."

Jim could hear Doug quietly sobbing.

"Doug, often the test of courage is not to die but to live. I'll be over in a few minutes. Meet me at the door."

Ten minutes later, Doug opened the door and Jim quietly walked in. Doug led him into his study where two chairs were positioned in front of a fireplace. Doug had a fire burning, and both men sat quietly looking into the fire. Doug then began to tell Jim, in total confidence, about the package, knowing that Jim wouldn't reveal this information, not even to Holly, his wife. He needed a confidante to help bear this burden with him and perhaps offer an opinion from a layman's perspective. Sometimes a perspective from someone outside their field was good.

"Doug, we don't know how this situation will play out, but God certainly does. He knows who has Cynthia, what this person's plans are with her, where Cynthia is, and what the outcome will be. Unfortunately, God doesn't speak to us and share that information. He just wants us to trust Him and know that it is in His hands. God tells us that His eye is on the sparrow, and He watches over us humans so much more. So if He takes care of the beasts of the fields, He will take care of each one of us. He knows where we are and what we need. Right now, all we can do is ask that God give Cindy peace and courage, and that God will intervene in this case and bring her home safely. If that is not His plan for Cynthia, Doug, He will be putting your faith and trust in Him to the test. He put Job's life to the test, and Job ended by saying, 'The Lord giveth, and the Lord taketh away. Blessed be the name of the Lord.' So have your soul prepared for anything, Doug."

"I'm not sure I'm a good man like Job, Jim. I don't know if I can pass the test."

"Trust me, Doug. You can. Cindy can too. Leave all of this in God's hands. Meanwhile Holly and I and the rest of the church are praying for your strength and courage, and will continue to hold you up in prayer."

The two men meditated on those words for awhile. In the darkest hours, Doug could count on Jim who was as close to him as a brother to bring peace to his heart when he felt he was crumbling. Doug couldn't let his children see him falling apart. Jim quietly left, and Doug locked the door and returned to his bedroom, turning off all the lights as he quietly slipped into bed. Alone.

As Doug lay in bed pondering the events of the last three days, he heard a quiet tapping on his bedroom door. The door cracked open and Doug heard Paul whisper softly, *"Dad, may I come in?"*

"Sure, son."

"Dad, I'm scared for Mom. I'm really scared."

"Me too, Paul."

"Dad, I need you to be honest with me. What makes Sgt. Parker think Taylor and I may be in danger?"

"Someone has invaded our home, son. We're not sure if it was a random choice or if this person deliberately selected our family. That's a possibility that has to be considered."

"But up until today, we weren't confined to the house. What changed? Officer Preston and Sgt. Parker's demeanor has gotten more austere, and you look even more troubled since Wednesday. I think you know more than what you're telling us. Am I right, Dad?"

"Perhaps, son, but I need you to trust me."

"I do, Dad, but I'm 19 years old. I'm an adult now. I can handle the truth more than I can handle the unknown. I don't want to be left out of what's going on." He spoke with such maturity and earnest honesty that Doug was tempted to tell Paul about the package, but on Sgt. Parker's advisement, he stepped back from the situation and obeyed his order to not include the kids.

"Let's get some rest, son. Tomorrow I'm going to the office and study records of criminals whom I helped send to prison. It's possible that someone with a vendetta has recently been paroled and wants to hurt me. We're considering every possibility."

"Do you think that's what's happening?"

"All I'm saying is that it's a possibility."

"Okay, Dad, but if I can help, I'll do anything."

"I know, son. Your mother and I love you so much. Try to get some sleep."

"You too, Dad. Good night."

Paul slipped quietly out of the room and Doug listened as Paul's bedroom door quietly closed behind him. Despite all of his troubles, Doug had a lot to be grateful for.

CHAPTER 17

SEPTEMBER 9

D oug left for his office long before the kids had gotten up. He put the security system back on and made sure he spoke to the officer on duty outside.

Taylor was awakened by her cell phone going off.

"Hello?"

"Taylor. It's Tim. You haven't been in school. I saw the news last evening. What's going on?"

Taylor had just recently met Tim on campus and was semi-dating him. She had brought him to their house for Labor Day events with the family. She really liked him even though she got the impression her mom wasn't too keen on him. It wasn't like they were going to get married or anything. Taylor was so happy to have someone from "the outside" talk to her and care about what was happening in her life. She began to tell Tim what had happened to her mom and gave him a detail by detail description about the on-going investigation. He listened attentively and then responded, *"Your mom is such a nice lady. Why would anyone do this to her?"*

"That's what we're trying to figure out. There's been no caller asking for a ransom and no tips have come in. It's like the trail has gone cold."

"This has to be horrible for you, Taylor. When can I see you?"

"I don't really know. My brother Paul and I are confined to the house for awhile. There's a detective on duty outside our house guarding my brother and I, in fact."

"Can I come see you?"

"I don't think that would be such a good idea right now. I would have to ask my Dad."

"No, don't ask your dad, Taylor. He's got enough on his mind. It's just that I miss you so much and want to see you."

"Give me some time, Tim. I'll find a way to step out of Alcatraz and steal a few minutes away from the house to spend with my 'new best friend.' It would be good for me to get out of here for awhile and get some fresh air. I really need to vent. "

"Well, call me on my cell. If you can sneak off, maybe I can meet you somewhere down the street, and we can go to a nearby coffee shop and talk for awhile. I promise to get you back home before anyone even knows you're gone."

"Sounds good, Tim."

"Take care, Taylor."

"You, too."

She hung up and spent the next few minutes thinking about Tim. He was so nice, and she was so lucky to have run in to him on the very first day back on campus. It was obvious he had taken a special interest in her. He was studying engineering and, apparently, being an upper classmen his classes were no where near hers on campus.

CHAPTER 18

Doug went through at least 20 of his file cases, reviewing his notes on each one. He had Jean, his secretary, check their prison status. Mitch was at the desk next to his and was grabbing as many files doing the same. Many were career criminals, some repeat DUI's, some drug addicts who had violated parole once too many times for the judge and had been put away, some burglars. One was a highly respected lawyer who had scammed a number of older clients out of their life's savings. He thought he was too slick to get caught, and if he did get caught, he could beat the system. He didn't.

Doug was responsible for having caught a few repeat voyeurs and some who made pornography their life's work. The crimes were endless and diversified. Not much of a difference between big city crimes and those of the smaller cities. The imaginations of a deceitful heart are everywhere.

Getting frustrated Doug burst out, *"How do we know if our kidnapper is the perpetrator himself? Maybe it's a relative of his. Maybe he hired someone to do it. It's impossible to know what or who we're looking for."* Mitch and Jean remained silent, understanding the stress Doug was feeling. They could easily empathize with him. Mitch insisted they pause long enough to eat their carry-in lunches. Normally they would go out for lunch, taking at least an hour while engaging in conversation that usually revolved around their families, particularly their wives. Mitch remained silent and allowed Doug to take the lead. Doug was unusually quiet and pensive. Mitch respected that.

"We're going to get this guy, Doug. Don't lose hope." With that Mitch returned to his desk and pulled out the next ten files. Doug did the same.

CHAPTER 19

Doug asked Jean to call Sgt. Parker and see if they got any results from some of the DNA or investigative tests.

Sgt. Parker got on the line immediately. *"Hi, Doug, how are you doing?"*

"I could be better, as you can imagine."

"I was just going to call you in a few minutes anyway, so I'm glad you called, Doug. Your Honda Accord was clean. Apparently our perp wore gloves and is either bald or wore a cap. The blood found in the trunk matched Cynthia's, along with strands of hair found. She was definitely in that trunk. One tire track that was tested, proved that another car was parked next to the Honda Accord. It was a worn Firestone 2156016 tire that could be used on a 2007 Ford Taurus SEL or Dodge Intrepid or any number of other cars. We're going to check out recent stolen cars in the area and see if we come up with anything, but we can pretty much deduct that Cynthia was transferred from one car to the other, which points, most likely, to her being alive—at least at that point. Otherwise, he probably would have left her body in her own car trunk. That's the good news."

"So what's the bad news?"

"It will take several more days to find out where the package was mailed from and to see whether prints can be taken off the panties."

CHAPTER 20

There was no light in the shed except for what little came through a small vent near the floor. Cynthia had had nothing to eat or drink since this ordeal began. She was dying of thirst and even though she was a nervous wreck, she was hungry. Her main concern was getting free so she could warn her children of their impending danger. If she could get hold of Doug, he would know exactly what to do. The trouble was making all of that happen. Unless she could escape, everyone was in danger.

She sat down in front of the vent and began to slide the rope back and forth on the metal slats. If she could get her arms free, she could untie her feet and escape. She tried moving her arms vertically for awhile, but nothing seemed to be happening with the rope. Then she tried moving her arms horizontally back and forth trying to wear the rope down or weaken it. Her arms were numb from being in that tied position for what had to be at least 72 hours. Her shoulder was also hurting her, but she could move it, so her arm must be in the socket. As painful and tiring as it was, she couldn't give up. Her life depended upon being able to escape. She was sure of that.

She had heard this guy lock the door from the outside. She couldn't feel a door knob on the inside nor could she figure out in the dark how to open this door if she did get her arms and legs freed. One step at a time, Cynthia. She could never fit through the small vent at the bottom.

So she knew the only way out was through that door. If she could at least break the vent, maybe she could yell for help or be able to look around to get a feel for the terrain.

Speed was important for she didn't know how soon he would be back. She assumed he left to go get something to eat, but perhaps he was kidnapping Taylor or Paul. Panic welled up inside her. With more urgency, she moved her arms back and forth, trying to break the rope. *Dear God, please get me out of here alive. Please!*

CHAPTER 21

Paul had always been a runner for his school teams. He had run track and cross country in high school. He ran track for Ohio State University and was always running to stay in shape. One day that goes by without running is a step backward in the conditioning process. Even when he was a little kid, his mom would have him run with her. It seemed so natural. When he was in high school running on the track team, he and his mom would go to the park and run together. He loved it when he could finally outrun her, but they had fun. When they tired, they would sit on a bench or on top of a hill and look out at the beautiful scenery and just talk. Mom was easy to talk to. She was fun, and all of the guys on the team loved her. She made all of his friends feel special. Many memories flooded his soul as he thought back on those track meets. Mom was always in the stands cheering him on. She was the best!

He needed desperately to go for a run. It was a stress reliever, and he certainly felt stress. With the police officer outside their home and making rounds, it would be more difficult to make it out of the house without being seen. More difficult but not impossible.

He was almost twenty years old—a grown man. He was six feet one, athletic. He lived on his own in an apartment in Columbus with no supervision. He was old enough to drink—well, almost— if he so chose, and he was old enough to fight in the war. He was majoring in biology at OSU and had a good head on his shoulders. He was disciplined and goal-oriented. He could go for a run and be back before anyone would even know he was gone.

Dad was over protective of him right now. That was understandable, but he could protect himself. It was Taylor who needed protecting. He watched carefully to see how often the police officer walked around their house. It had been every 20 minutes. He decided that as soon as the officer returned to his squad car, Paul would jump out of a window in the back and go for a run. He would need Taylor's cooperation, so he waited for her to come downstairs from her bedroom.

When she finally came down, he proposed a deal with her.

CHAPTER 22

Paul began. *"Taylor, I know we are both going stir crazy sitting in this house and that we both need to vent a little."*

"You can say that again. I am so worried about Mom I'm going crazy. I need to get away from the house if just for an hour to escape from it all."

"Well, you know we aren't allowed and that Dad would be upset. With the police officer outside, it makes it almost impossible to do so, especially since he walks around the house about every 20 minutes or so. So, here's what I was thinking. I need to go for a run. Mom would understand even if Dad wouldn't. It is my way of releasing stress. So I thought if you'd watch and make sure the officer was still in his car, I would jump out the kitchen window and take a 15 minute jaunt or so and then sneak back into the house. He wouldn't even know I was ever gone. No one would know. You close the window for me as soon as I jump out and I'll call you on my cell phone and have you tell me when the coast is clear, and then open the window for me so I can get in quickly and undetected.

"Okay, but what about me?"

"Well, you can call a friend and sneak a short visit if you get back here before being detected or before Dad comes home. Is that fair?"

"Yes."

"Okay. Now I just watched the officer circle around the house about 5 minutes ago, so you peak out the window and make sure he's still there."

"He's still in his car, Paul."

"Good. So when I jump out the window, you shut it for me and stay by the cell phone so you can tell me when the coast is clear. Then open the kitchen window so I can get back into the house quickly. Got it?"

"Yes."

"All right. I'm out of here. See you in a jiff!"

Paul jumped out the window with such agility and disappeared into the woods behind their house. As soon as he was in the clear, he knew his way through the path in the woods that led to the neighborhood several blocks away from their home. Just the brisk fresh air invigorated him and cleared his head. He tried not to think about his mother, which is all he had thought about for the last four days. He felt almost brain dead. He jogged the same route he had jogged with his mother hundreds of times while growing up. It was a safe neighborhood. He deleted everything from his memory for this one run, hoping to rejuvenate himself. Sooner or later, he needed to take a more active role in helping his father search for his mom. But for this moment in time, he blocked the situation out and took deep breaths while sprinting down the street. For the past twenty-five minutes his worries had dissipated. He needed to be making his way back home.

A branch snapped and he was sure he heard something. He stopped running, not making a move. He listened, waiting to hear movement. He looked quickly in all directions of the dark, dense woods to sense movement, but there was none. His mind, undoubtedly, was playing tricks on him. Before coming out of the woods, he called Taylor on her cell.

"Is the coast clear?"

"The officer just walked around the house and is heading for his car. Wait another minute. I'll tell you when it's safe to come out."

This was pretty slick the way this was working out, Paul thought. It was an ingenious plan. He felt so much better—mentally more prepared to face the circumstances head on.

"Okay, Paul. I have the window open. Make your move."

Paul ran out of the woods and straight for the open kitchen window. One quick leap with his long legs and he was standing in the kitchen, and no one but Taylor would know. Mission successful. He even felt close to his mother while on his run. It was like she was his guardian angel watching over him. If only he could do the same for her. Confidence was high. Paul looked at the clock on the stove. It was 7:45 p.m. Dad was expected home around 9 p.m. Taylor could pull this off, too, but she would have to watch the time, for sure.

CHAPTER 23

"Tim?"

"Taylor, it's you. I'm so glad you called. When can I see you?"

"Actually, that's why I'm calling. Things are so guarded around here, I'm going to have to sneak out of my house to meet you."

"Okay, so how and when and where?"

"Well, I'm going to have to jump out the kitchen window and run into the woods. I'm going to take a path that will bring me out onto Raber Road. If you could be there in your car waiting for me at the curb—at the corner of Raber and Dennison Avenue—I can get in the car and maybe we could go to the donut shop down the street and talk for a few minutes. Do you know where I'm talking about?"

"I'm sort of familiar with the area now, but I have a GPS in my car, so I'll be able to find it. When do you want me to meet you?"

"How about in ten minutes?"

"I'll be there."

The police officer had completed making his surveillance around the house and had returned to his car. Paul helped her out the kitchen window and reminded her to make it quick

"You've got to get home before Dad does or we're both in a lot of trouble. Call me before you step out of the woods so that I can check to see that it's safe. I'll help you through the window. Whatever you do, don't lose track of the time, Taylor. Be careful."

"You don't have to treat me like a baby, bro. I can take care of myself."

"I know you can, but I'm your big brother, so I have to watch out for you a little. So where are you going?"

"I'm just meeting Tim in front of the Snyder home there at Raber and Dennison. He'll drive us to the donut shop. We'll talk and have a donut, and I'm back before you know it."

"Okay. Don't forget Dad doesn't want us telling everyone all the details about Mom's disappearance."

"I know. I know. Tim wouldn't tell anyone anyway. He's not even from around here, so he doesn't know that many people to tell. So long!"

Paul watched her run into the woods, eager to meet her friend Tim. He wasn't sure if the word *boyfriend* was exactly in order, but she seemed happy to be meeting him. She needed to vent, that was for sure. She was so emotional and had been crying on and off for four days. She needed a stress releaser. He hoped her sneak trip would be pulled off without a hitch just as his was, but he worried that Taylor could botch the plan somehow, some way. Perhaps he shouldn't have suggested this as he watched Taylor run into the dense woods.

CHAPTER 24

W hen Taylor stepped out of the woods, she spotted Tim sitting in his car. He was on the cell phone talking to someone. As soon as he got into view, he immediately got off the phone and stepped out of the car. As soon as he put his strong arms around her, she felt safe and a peace came over her. He gave the best hugs in the whole wide world.

Tim opened the car door for her and handed her the seat belt. When he got in, he reached in the back seat and handed her a box of donuts and a latte. He started the car, and pulled away from the curb.

"I thought we were going to the donut shop."

"I was afraid we'd be rushed for time or that you might get into trouble, so I thought it best if we just drive to the park and eat in the car and talk."

"Oh. You're probably right. I just have to watch my time, though," Taylor admonished.

Tim parked the car at the end of the lot where the light was out. As they sat in the dark, she reached for a donut and began to drink her latte. He began to sip his coffee and eat a donut as well.

"So, what's been going on Taylor?"

"Tim, I'm so worried about my Mom. I don't want to believe anything bad has happened to her, but she wouldn't be gone this long if something hadn't happened. She would have called. There was definitely a struggle in our home, and there was blood in her bedroom. I . . . I . . ." she began to cry.

"Taylor, just relax. Don't talk. It's upsetting you. Just drink your latte and hold my hand. I want to be here for you . . . to comfort you." She sat in silence, unable to speak, sipping at her latte. Somewhat worried about her time, she wasn't really hungry for the donut now but the latte was comforting. Tim looked upon her with admiration and such empathy that she felt he truly understood what she was going through.

Taylor now understood what her mom meant when she explained how she and her dad could sit together in a room and never speak a word yet feel so much love and peace. Taylor looked out the window but things looked somewhat foggy.

She tried to speak. *" I guess it's all getting to me . . . I feel . . . emotionally . . . exhausted. Things seem to be getting . . . so blurry, Tim. I need to be . . . getting . . . home."*

The GHB that Tim had slipped into her drink worked faster than he had imagined. He had to work quickly. He had to follow the plan.

CHAPTER 25

"*Did you find the gun?*" the caller asked urgently.

"*I'm still working on that, but it's almost impossible searching in a cold, murky pond at night. Why couldn't you have thrown the gun in some bushes? It would have made it easier and quicker to retrieve.*"

"*Yes, but easier for A+ detectives to find. Remember, when you retrieve it, wipe it down. File the serial number off then take it to another state and bury it in a desolate, remote area where it can never be found. Do you understand?*"

"*I understand.*"

"*And you burned the bloody clothes?*"

"*Yes. They are disposed.*"

"*You need to hurry. I can only stall the situation another day or two. Is Cynthia okay?*"

"*She's fine. Don't worry. I've got it all under control.*"

"*Remember, no one is to get hurt. You help me, and you will have the money waiting in your account. The fewer times we talk, the better. Just get the job done so that everyone can get on with their lives.*"

"*Hmmmph!*"

"*What? Didn't I get you paroled several months early?*"

"*And for what? I've got no family to go to.*"

"*You've got your freedom and lots of money to live on comfortably for a long while.*"

"Call me when the evidence has been found, totally destroyed, and irretrievable. Got it?"

"Yes, boss."

Click.

Quinton was thrilled with how the events had played out so far. He would play by the boss's rules up to a point, and then he planned to change some of the rules. If his plan worked out, he would walk away the winner—indeed a rich man having satisfied his revenge and still have a relationship with one son.

CHAPTER 26

Having gone through case after case all day long, Doug felt he was no closer to figuring out which suspect would have held a grudge so deeply, he was willing to hurt Doug's family. It was time to call it a night.

He decided to call home before leaving. Paul answered on the first ring.

"Hello?"

"Hi, son. Is everything okay at the house?"

"Sure, Dad. We're fine."

"Good. Well, I'm leaving the office right now, so I should be home in about twenty minutes. Do you need me to stop at the store for anything?"

"Uh, yeah. I could sure use some caramel praline ice cream, Dad, and some Wheaties."

"Okay. I'll be home in thirty minutes. I'll update you guys when I get home."

Mitch decided to stay at the office to work just a little longer. He had just pulled up a file on a Quinton Reed that aroused some curiosity, and he wanted to review it.

As soon as Paul hung up from talking to his dad, he immediately called Taylor on her cell. She needed to get home and fast! She had already been gone longer than twenty-five minutes and was pressing her luck.

The phone rang but Taylor never picked up. He was forced to leave a message.

"Taylor, Dad is on his way home right now. I stalled him. He's stopping at Giant Eagle to pick up some ice cream and cereal, but you've got to get home NOW! He should be home in thirty minutes or less. Call me."

Paul turned off the kitchen lights and looked out the window. He tried to scan the dark woods to see if he could spot Taylor close by, ready to pop out from behind a tree. Nothing. He waited five more minutes and still no response from Taylor.

"Darn it, Taylor. Pick up!"

He called her again.

He should never have let her leave the house. Why couldn't she follow directions? Girls— well, sisters—were exasperating! She always knew how to pull his chain. Now was certainly not the time to play games. He called her cell again.

"Come on, Taylor. Pick up. You've got to get home. You've got to!"

CHAPTER 27

Doug pulled into the driveway and walked over to the detective on duty outside. He leaned into the passenger's window to get a report from the officer.

"No unusual occurrences, sir. All is quiet."

Thanking the officer for his watchful care over their home knowing it was a tedious duty, Doug entered the house carrying the ice cream, cereal, and a few more items on Doug's *"want list."* His comfort food.

"Hi, son."

"Hi, Dad."

"How did the search go today?"

"No case is screaming out at us. We don't have time on our side, but these searches don't move along quickly. If only a name would pop out of my subconscious mind, but it just isn't."

"So, where's Taylor?"

"I'm not sure."

"Taylor, there's a bowl of caramel praline ice cream sitting here in the kitchen with your name on it." Doug yelled up the stairs.

No response.

"Is she asleep, Paul?"

"I don't think so."

Doug climbed the stairs and knocked on Taylor's bedroom door. No response again. There was no light shining through the cracks of the door, so very gently he opened the door and peaked in. Her bed was made. He switched the light on but clearly she wasn't in the room. The bathroom door was open and unlit. Fear started to well up in Doug as he quickly descended the stairs. He had a frightened and troubled look on his face.

Finally Paul cried out and told his dad about his plan and how he hasn't been able to reach Taylor on her cell for the last thirty minutes.

In total disbelief that this could be happening, Doug hit Taylor's programmed number on his cell phone but was sent to the *leave a message* mode also. Doug switched from dad mode to cop mode. He had the police officer on duty step inside the house. Officer Trent was shocked to learn that not one but two of the teens he was assigned to protect had left the home under his watch and were undetected.

They did a thorough search of the house first and then questioned Paul about who Taylor was meeting and where. A missing persons was put out on Taylor, and Paul and Doug got in Doug's car and drove to the Raber and Dennison Avenue intersection where Paul believed Taylor was planning to meet Tim Smith. No cars were parked at the curb in either direction. They drove to the Dunkin Donut shop nearby and inquired of Taylor and Tim. No young couple of that description was seen there the entire evening. They were shown a picture of Taylor. No one inside the shop had seen her. They seemed very sure.

Meanwhile, Paul kept calling Taylor's cell phone. Still nothing.

While in the car, Doug inquired to Paul about Tim Smith.

"Are you sure she was meeting him, Paul?"

"She called out his name while talking to him on her cell, Dad."

"Do you know anything about him, Paul?"

"Just what you know. When he spent Labor Day with us, he said he was a junior studying mechanical engineering at KSU. He wasn't from around here, as I recall, but I don't think he ever said where he was from."

"I don't remember, either, but I do remember your mom mentioning to me she didn't trust him."

"Why was that?"

"As I recall, when we were outside in the backyard grilling, he went inside the house. Said he needed to use the bathroom. When Cynthia went inside to bring out the condiments, he was coming downstairs."

"So?"

"Well, she sensed that instead of using the bathroom, he was nosing around. Why wouldn't he have used the bathroom there off the kitchen?"

"Well, maybe he didn't know about the half bath off the kitchen."

"Taylor told him where it was."

"Well, maybe he wanted more privacy."

"Yes, that could be true. But could he possibly have been casing the house or getting acquainted with the layout because he planned to return at another time?"

"Gosh, Dad. That's stretching your imagination pretty far, isn't it?"

"Is it, Paul? First your mom is missing and now Taylor appears to be missing, and the last person we think saw Taylor was Tim Smith."

Paul pondered that for a few minutes.

Several police cars arrived at the Conrad home and the police began canvassing the woods with bright flashlights. It was possible Taylor never made it out of the woods, but then, wouldn't Tim have attempted to contact someone at the house when Taylor never showed up or perhaps drive around the house out of curiosity? In Tim's defense, had he tried to call Taylor, he, too, wouldn't have been able to get through to her if he was innocent.

Innocent before proven guilty, unless you are the father of a missing daughter.

CHAPTER 28

Doug pulled into the driveway and told Paul to stay in the house and lock all of the doors. They first checked to see if Taylor had returned to the house while they were gone. She hadn't.

Doug took a flashlight from the garage and headed for the woods behind their house. Paul begged to come along.

"Someone needs to be here in case Taylor returns or tries to call."

"Okay, Dad. I'm . . . I'm so sorry about all of this."

"We'll talk when I get home, son, but for now pray that Taylor is safe and just being Taylor. Meanwhile, snoop in her bedroom and see if you can find any information on Tim Smith—a phone number, a picture of him, anything. Check her purses, wallet, etc.

"Be careful, Dad."

Paul looked out the kitchen window into the woods. He saw lights moving in all directions from the flashlights of the four or five searchers.

Tears started streaming down his face. *"Please don't be in those woods, Taylor. Please."*

CHAPTER 29

Doug knew these woods better than anyone. He knew which way Taylor would have gone to meet someone at Raber and Dennison. He headed in that direction. He could hear the police officers conversing to one another as they spread out.

Doug would stop every so often to listen for sounds of breathing or moaning. He would call out Taylor's name but to no avail. He saw no signs of Taylor—not her shoes, torn clothing, nothing. That was good. He started to follow his steps back to where he began. He saw even more lights visible in the woods. Four of the neighbor men, including John Rogers, Lucy's husband, had heard what was happening and came to join the search. What wonderful friends and neighbors he had. He felt blessed, but through all of that, his heart was gripped with panic. He was, after all, the only known man in the country whose wife and daughter were missing . . . and foul play was the probable cause.

CHAPTER 30

Sgt. Parker called to say he was on his way over to their home. Officer Trent was filling out a report in his squad car. Doug walked into the house an emotional volcano. How could his kids deliberately disobey him when the situation was so grave? How could this officer not be watching more closely? And where was God? Why was He letting this happen to his family? Doug began to cry uncontrollably from utter fear, not knowing where his wife was and now his baby girl. Who had them? What were they going through? Would he see them again?

Paul had never seen his dad sob like this before. How could he have failed his dad so miserably? It was his responsibility to protect his sister, and he didn't do it. He loved and respected his father so much. Why did he disobey and bring such grief to his dad? How could he have been so naïve? He didn't realize the possible ramifications of stepping out of the house unattended. He never realized the gravity of the situation until now. His fear and guilt were overwhelming.

Sgt. Parker arrived and was led into the living room. Mitch arrived as soon as he had heard, and everyone was in agreement that Pastor Pascoe needed to be there also. Doug was shutting down emotionally, and they were going to need him to think and help put the pieces to the puzzle together.

News reporters arrived, hanging out in the front yard with cameras ready, demanding a story. No one was talking, but something BIG had happened. Now even more police officers had arrived to stand outside the house while others made their way to the woods. Slick reporters slipped through the yards of neighbors to make their way into the woods and assess what was happening. Had a body been found?

Pastor Pascoe arrived and was escorted into the house. He immediately went to Doug and embraced him.

"Why? Why, Jim?"

"How are you doing, Doug?"

"I'm . . . at my . . . . wit's . . . . end." He was weeping so bitterly he was almost inaudible. Pastor Pascoe kept his embrace as his dear friend sobbed and had a death grip on his shoulders.

"When you get to your wit's end, you'll find God lives there too, Doug."

"I've got to . . . figure this out, but . . . nothing is coming to . . . me."

"The task ahead of us is never as great as the Power behind us," said Pastor Pascoe, but he, nevertheless, felt so helpless. Words could not provide the emotional strength and courage that Doug would need. Only the Holy Spirit could do that for Doug. He whispered a prayer for Doug and kept holding on.

CHAPTER 31

Taylor woke up in the trunk of Tim's car, both hands and feet were secured by a rope. Confused, she called out.

"Tim . . . help me! What's happening? Help me! Someone . . . please help me!"

Tim heard her anguished, frightened cries. She started kicking the top of the trunk lid and he feared someone would either hear her or see the trunk lid move and get curious. He was determined to get her to the required destination and safely, but he would need to sedate her again before getting on the turnpike.

He took the first exit off the highway and found a country road that seemed to lead to nowhere. It was quite late, so darkness was on his side. He pulled onto the road and drove for about 1/8 of a mile and then stopped. There was a woods on one side and a field on the other, with nothing in front or in back of him. He got out of the car and opened the back door of his car. Bending down, he picked up a cloth and poured chloroform on it, soaking it. He unlocked the trunk door and lifted the door up. Taylor was kicking and trying her best to get out, but she was so confined by the ropes, she had little ability to move.

"Help!" she screamed to the top of her lungs.

"Taylor, I'm not going to hurt you. No one is going to hurt you. We just need you out of commission for a little bit. Your mom is safe. I'm going to take you to see your mom, but you need to stop screaming.

Everything is going to work out okay for you and your mom. Just trust me, Taylor."

Having said that, he put the cloth over her nose and mouth and a few seconds later, Taylor passed out. Doing such a thing was not in his comfort zone, but he wanted to please his father. He finally had a chance to have a relationship with his father—something he had never had his entire life. Nothing was going to stop him from that. His father had asked him to get inside the Conrad home so he could describe the layout for him and to later deliver Taylor— these two favors with a promise no one would get hurt. It would mean a lot of money for his dad, and he could finally get back on his feet and make a life for himself. He wanted that for his dad and for him.

CHAPTER 32

A call was made to Kent State University to the Dean of Men. Sgt. Parker asked that he pull up every Tim Smith on record as a student there. He was particularly looking for a Tim Smith who was a junior in mechanical engineering. He needed to see pictures of each one of the Tim Smiths with a present address and phone number for each young man. Pull the files of each one. He would need a student I.D., a license plate number, next of kin, etc. He would be arriving on campus in thirty minutes.

"Doug, I need you to come with me to Kent State and identify the correct Tim Smith. Can you do that?"

"Yes, I would remember what he looked like even though I only met him that one day," he said.

It took about forty minutes before Sgt. Parker drove onto the campus and began their search for the Administration Building which also happened to house the Dean of Men. They were directed to the second floor in a spacious and rather posh office. Dean Walters met both men in the lobby and immediately escorted them to his office. They were asked to step to a desk where the dean had spread the pictures of fifteen Tim Smiths out accompanied by a file on each young man. There were no Tim Smiths, however, that were juniors who concentrated their studies in mechanical engineering. As Doug's eyes glanced across all fifteen pictures, not one looked like the Tim Smith he knew.

Dejected, the two men thanked the dean and returned to their car. As they sat in the parking lot, Doug suggested they drive to Taylor's apartment off campus where Taylor shared a place with two other girls. It was1 a.m. and as badly as they hated awaking the girls and perhaps terrifying them, they knew they couldn't spare hours. Taylor may not have that kind of time. They drove directly to her apartment, which took them about fifteen minutes. It was a very tiny white Cape Cod home. Both men stepped out of the car and walked the four steps up to the front porch and rang the doorbell.

There was no response. Doug rang the doorbell again while Sgt. Parker knocked on the door. A light in the back of the house came on and the men could hear some shuffling in the house. The porch light came on and a girl demurely peaked through the thin, lacy curtains.

"Akron Police. We need to ask you girls some questions." He held his badge out so that the girl could see it.

"Just a minute," she called out. She returned to the back of the house and apparently put on a bathrobe. Another girl also came to the door wearing a bath robe. The second girl recognized Mr. Conrad and the door opened.

"Mr. Conrad, is everything okay?"

"Hi, Tiffany. I'm afraid it isn't." he responded with such sadness in his voice.

"Why are you here?" the other girl asked.

"We're sorry to bother you and scare you at this late hour, but Taylor is missing, and we believe she may be with a boy named Tim Smith. Do you know where or how he can be reached?" Sgt. Parker asked.

"No. You mean Taylor is missing as in being kidnapped?"

"Possibly. She was supposed to be meeting Tim and hasn't been seen since," Doug revealed to the girls who were friends with Taylor.

"What do you girls know about this Tim Smith?" asked Sgt. Parker.

"Not much of anything, really. Taylor talked about him once in awhile. He never came here to pick her up but once. She had lunch with

him on campus once. He's studying mechanical engineering, I think,"
said Tiffany.

"Do you remember what his classification is?"

"I believe he is a junior. Taylor never had any classes with him or anything, but he would walk her to her class occasionally."

"Can you describe for us what he looks like?" asked Sgt. Parker.

Both girls looked at each other and began debating height and weight.

"I would say he was about 6 feet, 175 lbs." said Haley.

"I'd say he was more like 5 feet nine inches, 155 lbs." said Tiffany.

"Keep going."

"He had short, brown hair, parted on the side, I believe."

"Wait," said Tiffany. *"I think I took a picture of Tim and Taylor on my cell phone while sitting on the couch here a few weeks ago."*

"If you have that picture, that would help us tremendously, Tiffany." said Doug.

Tiffany went to her bedroom to retrieve her cell phone. She returned to the living room pushing a button on her cell phone that was bringing up the various pictures she had taken. She finally came to one.

"Oh, here it is," handing her phone to Mr. Conrad. He looked at the picture and confirmed that that was the Tim Smith he knew. This was the BIG break that Sgt. Parker and Doug were hoping for.

Sgt. Parker asked if he could borrow her cell phone for a day or two until the police could download this picture. Tiffany agreed to it, of course, and expressed her deepest sympathy to Mr. Conrad about Taylor. Both Tiffany and Haley had tears in their eyes, and expressed their love and concern for Taylor.

Sgt. Parker admonished both girls to lock the doors behind them when they left and to keep this meeting private. It would most likely reach the news on TV, but they were asked not to discuss this with anyone.

"If you hear from Taylor or Tim or learn anything about what's been going on, please call us immediately." Both men handed the girls their business card.

CHAPTER 33

The entire woods had been searched thoroughly, and the police were convinced there was no body in the woods. Wherever Taylor was, it was somewhere other than these woods. Sgt. Parker offered Doug his condolences and assured him they would be working on the case around the clock.

The news stations had picked up pieces of the story from the police band radio but weren't able to get even a quote from Sgt. Parker when he walked out of the house to his company car. The reporters, however, felt they had enough information to run with a story from comments made by neighbors who had been canvassing the woods behind the Conrad home.

Channel 3 began its 11 o'clock telecast with breaking news. *"Good evening. Another tragedy has hit the Douglas Conrad home. It appears yet another family member is missing—Nineteen year old daughter Taylor has been missing from their home since approximately 9 p.m. this evening. You will remember Detective Conrad's wife was abducted on Sept. 6 and the authorities have been searching for her with little clues to go on and with no success. Sgt. Parker who is in charge of this case has refused to provide any information in this second disappearance, but we can tell you that over ten police officers and neighbors have searched the woods behind the Conrad home for over two hours. The authorities are remaining tight lipped, so as soon as more details unfold, we will bring you the update. This is Erin Wright from Channel 3 News, reporting from Green, Ohio."*

CHAPTER 34

Sgt. Parker took Tiffany's cell phone back to the department and had his experts download the picture of Tim Smith. They were going to have to post his photo on television and let the public identify this person for them, going nationally if need be. Every police officer on every beat would be given a copy of his photo as well as Taylor's and be on the alert to find one or both of these individuals.

Was it possible that Taylor had run off with Tim Smith willingly? Perhaps Doug and Paul Conrad had miscalculated her feelings for this young man. Did she need to get away from the pressure? Doug hadn't shared Cynthia's skepticism about this boy when he visited their home on Labor Day. Was it women's intuition or merely parental protection? A lot of man hours had already been put into finding Taylor. He was hoping for his sake that she was merely a runaway. So far Mayor Stanwick insisted on giving the Conrad case priority. He had indicated he needed to get Doug Conrad back on the trail to exonerate his nephew from suspicion of the McGrady/ Stover murders.

There was something about this case that was so troubling to him. He couldn't put his finger on it, but he knew Doug Conrad long enough to know he was devastated by the events of the past days and the havoc it was playing on his life. He could only imagine what this nice man was going through. The man would be destroyed if he lost both his wife and daughter. They couldn't let that happen. They just couldn't.

CHAPTER 35

Steve Stanwick had been mayor of Akron for four years and had prided himself on working for the hard—working class citizens of his mid size town. He had grown up here and had numerous contacts and resources. He was well liked by the people of Akron and made himself readily available to them. He was hard working himself and highly respected by the city workers and other subordinates who answered to him.

He was fifty-five years old with a lovely wife. They were unable to have children. His twin brother, Ed, had been transferred with his job to Chicago and his son Allen came to live with them while going through law school at the University of Akron. Steve came to love Allen as if he were his own son and couldn't have been more proud of him. Allen became a lawyer, specializing in probate and trust administration at his father-in-law's law firm. He had set up countless wills, guardianships, estate planning, and asset protection for the citizens of the Summit County area and other surrounding counties. His knowledge in the field was irrefutable as was his greedy and cunning reputation. He no longer had to advertise, getting most of his business through referrals.

His father-in-law, Dan Dunford had seen early on that Allen was a guy with less than noble work ethics and was avarice. Mr. Dunford owned a prestigious law firm and had worked hard to build that reputation on strong values. However, he was never able to instill those same values in Allen when he came aboard right out of law school and had married his daughter. Allen had grown up having the finest in life—the best schools, the fastest cars, and had a father who had fought most of his battles for him. He knew Ed. Ed made his son's cheating accusations go away, arranged for his son to make first string on any sport he played, and stuck up for him on occasion when he was sure his son had even lied to him. He taught his son how to be refined and cultured and to be a smooth talker. He taught him to respect people who had money. But Allen always seemed to stray from the strait and narrow path, always going down the easy road or taking the path of least resistance. He always wanted something for nothing, and he knew how to impress the women. He was articulate, suave, and handsome. While Dan would do almost anything for his daughter, he refused to make Allen a partner in his law firm, although she had pressured him on several occasions to do so. The paralegals were preparing Allen's briefs while he would make the stirring deliveries when a will was contested. As a result, he won a majority of his cases, so he was, generally speaking, an asset to Dunford, Ruhlin, and Rucker Law Firm.

There had been no known problems that Steve had been aware of regarding Allen until the deaths of Mrs. McGrary and her caregiver. Mrs. McGrary's estate had been represented by Allen. Mrs. McGrary had been murdered along with her caregiver, Madeline Stover, who was hired to care for Mrs. McGrary around the clock. Mrs. McGrary was eighty –six years old, had been a widow for more than twenty years, and had been childless, although she had one niece whom she wished to be the sole recipient of her vast wealth. She was very frail physically but was still of sound mind and had an acute memory, especially an acumen for figures. That surely was attributed to her thirty years as an accountant with Firestone Tire and Rubber Company.

According to the Beacon Journal, Mrs. McGrary and her caregiver were found shot to death two days after their murders, according to the coroner. A mailman became suspicious when neither the mail nor the newspapers had been picked up for two days. He knocked on the door and then peeked through a window when no one answered. That's when he saw Mrs. McGrary in her chair with blood all over her clothing. He then saw Madeline on the floor nearby, and she appeared to be dead. He called the authorities. The investigation is still on-going, but Allen became a *"person of interest"* when it was discovered that he was the beneficiary of much of Mrs. McGrary's vast estate and lucrative investments rather than the niece. Thus, a possible motive. However, the home had been mildly ransacked in an attempt to appear robbery was the motive. There had been no forced entry into the home.

Allen did own a gun that he was not able to produce, which was the type and caliber that was used on Mrs. McGrary and Madeline Stover. The gun was needed to either prove him innocent or guilty. Allen had driven to Chicago to visit his folks on the very day of the murders, but when the time of death was established, it was possible that Allen could have been in the area and had time to commit the crimes. Of course, Allen denied vehemently that he had anything to do with their deaths, and the Mayor believed him.

Allen arrived unexpectedly at Mayor Stanwick's office and demanded to see his uncle.

"I'm sorry, but Mr. Stanwick asked not to be disturbed this afternoon," said the receptionist. Allen ignored her and walked into Uncle Steve's office. Steve Stanwick looked up as Allen closed the door behind him. Steve called his receptionist.

"I'm so sorry, Mr. Stanwick. He just walked right into your office and disregarded my warning not to go in." "That's all right, Ann. Allen is my nephew, so he can get by with it. We don't wish to be disturbed, so please hold all of my calls. I want no disruptions for awhile. Thank you."

Steve's demeanor changed almost immediately as he looked up at Allen.

"I told you not to come see me nor to call until the problem has been resolved. What part of that don't you understand?"

"I need closure fast, and I'm not hearing about any progress. I need to know what's going on." Allen was clearly panicking.

"You listen to me and listen hard. I have stuck my neck out for you—literally my entire career—both personally and professionally. I have loved you like my own son, but you have me up to my eyeballs in possible obstruction of justice and perhaps accessory. I have used my power to take attention away from you—to distract this investigation and misdirect the authorities. You do anything to draw attention to yourself and to me, we will both live to regret this. Now get out of this office and don't come back here nor call me until things have died down. I'll let you know when the problem has been resolved."

CHAPTER 36

Cynthia was beginning to lose hope. She had lost track of time, but she knew when it was night time, despite not having windows. It became quite cool in the shed compared to the days when it felt warm and stuffy. She was starving. Her abductor hadn't given her anything to eat nor drink since he kidnapped her. She could feel herself becoming dehydrated. She was starting to feel weak and could barely urinate. Fortunately she was in excellent health and if she didn't exhaust her energy foolishly, she would reserve her strength if the opportunity arose to escape. She guestimated that this was her third day in captivity. Why the long interval between his visits was disconcerting. Was he demanding a ransom for her? He said he was going to kill her, so why the wait if that were true?

She had plenty of time to think. She could only imagine what Doug was thinking and feeling. Controlled rage and probably working around the clock to find her. She felt his presence with her here. She could feel him, sense him. She wept as she thought about the anguish Doug and the kids were going through. If the outcome does turn out badly, the kids would move on with their lives, but Doug . . . he would be completely devastated and lost, despite the strong demeanor he had always displayed publicly and professionally. Paul would be going crazy with fear and concern, wanting to help, and Taylor would be hysterical and so worked up she would be of little use. Hopefully people were offering comfort to her family as well as being on the lookout for her.

She wondered if her abduction had made the news and what was being said. What were her friends and neighbors doing to help? Were they bringing in food to sustain her family? Was the family remembering to feed Snuggles?

Again, she felt enraged that this man could trespass on her property and just forcibly take her. He definitely frightened her. She had been left alone for a very long time. She assumed he would be coming back, but as long as she was alone, she felt safe. That would give someone time to find her. She had passed the hours by praying— praying for her safety and that for her family, for the police that they would find her soon, and that the outcome would be better than most outcomes she'd heard about or read in the news.

Doug was the last person she thought about before drifting off to a light sleep and the first person she thought of when she awoke. When she closed her eyes, she could feel Doug's presence and see him with such clarity it was as though she could reach out and touch him. She envisioned his beautiful smile, his warm embrace. She could hear his deep, commanding voice. He was and had always been the love of her life.

This entire event seemed so surreal. She could hardly believe this was happening to her, so she could only imagine the shock her family, friends, and good neighbors were feeling.

She was helpless sitting in this shed. She was totally dependent on others to find her. She felt numb physically. She was tired and exhausted, but she felt so many different emotions coursing through her. No matter how this ended, she knew God was in control, and He was watching over her. Of that she was certain.

Just then she heard a car pull up and the car door slam. All of her peace suddenly disappeared.

CHAPTER 37

Ramona was on her way home from work. Since her divorce nearly 15 years ago, she was forced out of her housewife role and into being a part-time clerk at Dillard's. She thought when she married that she would be a stay at home mom, raising her children just as her mom had done. But after the divorce with few skills to boast of, she frantically searched for a badly needed full-time job.

The problem was, she hadn't married a guy like her dad. Her dad had been a tire builder for Firestone Tire and Rubber Company for thirty-eight years and had eeked out a decent living for her and her brother. There wasn't a lot of extra money to spare but needs were always met. They had a no frills house, but her mom could stretch every dime like nobody she knew. Their home exuded in love, however, and was always quiet and peaceful. She dreamed that life would be like that for her after she grew up and moved away.

After high school graduation, she was sauntering through a neighborhood park with her girlfriend when they met two boys. The one boy caught her eye immediately. He was tall, dark, and handsome and had a daredevil spirit in him. She found him fun and exciting. He was nothing like the other boys she knew from school. He was a bit of a show off, however, and loved attention. After they started dating, she realized he was a good athlete and had a strong, competitive nature to go along with it. She viewed him as a wild, untamed mustang who demanded to be his own master. In her young nineteen years, Ramona interpreted those qualities in him as being self confident and aggressive; therefore, she believed he could be anything he wanted to be. Theirs was a worldwind romance. He swept her off her feet.

He tried some moves on her, but she always managed to keep him in tow. She promised her mom there'd be no sex before marriage, and a promise made was a promise kept. However, fondling was a different issue, and she felt flattered and desired when his hands slid down her back and he pressed close to her—too close for comfort. He begged for more, but she reminded him of her promise to her mother. She had never felt love like this before and knew before too long, he would propose, and she was ready to say *yes*.

Ramona sensed her folks didn't like him all that much, especially her dad, but when they saw how happy she was, they backed off and didn't say much.

As soon as he got his first full-time job in road construction, he proposed. They found a one bedroom apartment to rent and one month later they were married by a justice of the peace at his insistence with no family members present. Her parents had a hard time accepting that, but she felt they would come around. They would have no choice, for she was now legally Mrs. Quinton Reed.

CHAPTER 38

Ramona's goals were to get a full-time job so they could rent a larger apartment or acquire a mediocre down payment on a small house of their own. But Kalen was born ten months after they were married, followed by Kerry one year later and then Kevin. It was then she made the decision to have her tubes tied. The babies put such stress on Quinton that he became detached to the boys, blaming them for their financial woes.

Quinton took on as much over-time as he could although she never saw a difference in his paycheck. They were getting further and further behind in their bills.

When she questioned him about his paycheck, he told her construction had slowed down and there was nothing he could do. He began coming home later and later each passing day and was very drunk. Once again she confronted him about the unpaid bills, his drinking, and not spending any time with the babies. That's when he knocked her across the room and into the wall.

"Never tell me what to do or when to do it. Do you understand? Stop complaining, bitch, or you'll get more of this!"

And his promise stood the test of time. That was just the beginning of more to come. This wild mustang was unleashed and untamed.

CHAPTER 39

An eviction warning arrived one morning and Ramona was mortified and saw no answer to the dilemma she was in. Quinton came home from work early the next day declaring he had paid the next two months' rent and was taking the family out to dinner. He had received a bonus from work. Two days later he was arrested for petty theft.

As the years passed and Ramona looked back on her married life with Quinton, it was one big fiasco. Her parents had to bail them out of debt numerous times so that they had a roof over their heads. She, meanwhile, had bailed him out of jail for a myriad of crimes—road rage, work rage, resisting arrest, disorderly conduct, and theft. He had been a poor excuse for a husband. He was physically and verbally abusive to her, but usually he left the children alone. Many nights he never came home, and she never knew whether he was out committing another crime or was staying overnight with someone he met at the bars. Even though she had stayed with him, their marriage had been over for quite some time. She was the glue that kept the family together, with lots of help, of course, from her parents. Her sons probably missed having a father, but they never spoke openly about it. She never put Quinton down as a father or husband, but the children weren't stupid. They weren't blinded as to what was going on, and they had a healthy fear of him.

As more time went on, Quinton's crimes escalated. The courts were getting impatient with his recurring court appearances and his lame excuses; his lawyer admonished him that the courts were unlikely to continue offering community service and shorter jail sentences if his crime patterns continued.

CHAPTER 40

One day a man, an investigator, knocked on Ramona's door and asked to speak to Quinton who wasn't home at the time, so he asked her lots of questions about Quinton. He was rather evasive about the crime involved, merely said it was about a *cold* case—robbery of a convenience store in the suburbs. She answered his questions amidst the boys watching TV and fighting over a toy in the living room. The baby was always an annoyance to the two older boys, and they were constantly picking on him and taking advantage of him. Ramona could tell by the investigator's questions that Quinton was a *person of interest* in this crime. She knew she would never lie or cover for Quinton, but she honestly couldn't remember where Quinton was on the day in question almost a year ago. Quinton had many different jobs throughout their marriage, and he had never resigned from any of them. It was not uncommon for him to miss work even though he left the house as though he were going. She knew never to question him about that either or it would result in some form of violence. She was so weary of him. She wanted out of this marriage, but she was afraid of what he would do if she tried to leave. She wouldn't miss him nor would the boys if he were out of their lives.

She figured one of these days he would break the law and be sent to prison, but she had no idea this case would be the clincher. Although the investigator didn't have a search warrant, she allowed him to look at

Quinton's gun collection. She provided where he worked when the crime had been committed. The investigator was very polite and pleasant and seemed delighted to chat with the boys. It was obvious he loved kids and had a kind heart. She seemed to have satisfied his curiosity and answered all of his questions. He left and she thought nothing more about it until the police came at 1:00 a.m. two mornings later with a search warrant, demanding to talk to Quinton. Without any hesitation, they read off his Miranda rights, handcuffed him, and arrested him for the murder of Dean Dutton, the proprietor of the 7 Eleven convenience store in Mogadore, Ohio, a suburb 10 miles from their home. Quinton didn't say a word but looked utterly surprised as they escorted him to the squad car. They also had a search warrant to confiscate one of his guns.

"Call my lawyer, Ramona! Now! I didn't do nothing and they're not going to pin anything on me. I'll sue the entire police department and own Akron when I'm done!" he screamed in total defiance and arrogance.

Quinton certainly had a mean streak, but never would she dream he would murder someone. She didn't want Kalen, Kerry, nor Kevin to be stereotyped as the *"sons of a murderer"* so she prayed that for once Quinton was telling the truth.

CHAPTER 41

Four months later, Quinton was sentenced to fifteen years to life for aggravated robbery and murder of the convenience store owner. Quinton was so sure that he had gotten by with the crime—after all, a year had passed since the crime and it seemed that there were no witnesses and no evidence to point to him. When police had seemingly allowed the case to get cold, Dutton's wife hired a private investigator to find her husband's killer. The investigator, Douglas Conrad, took the witness stand in court and explained how he was able to put the pieces to the puzzle together that led him to Quinton Reed. Once Reed's gun was seized, forensics did its job and Quinton knew he was facing a lengthy prison sentence. Plea bargaining had been denied.

Quinton had no intention of killing the store owner, but Dutton refused to turn over the money in the store cash register when ordered to. His defiance is what cost him his life. Quinton thought he was reaching for a gun, so he viewed the killing as one of *self defense,* even if the jury didn't concur with his reason for shooting the man.

As soon as Quinton established his residence at Lorain Correction Institute, he was served divorce papers. Not once did Ramona nor the boys come to visit him nor did they write to him. He wrote his sons numerous times but wasn't sure if they even knew he had written. Probably Ramona deliberately usurped the letters so that he would be nothing more than a faded memory. His anger festered as time went on.

He was determined to renew a relationship with his sons when he was released from prison. Ramona was a weak, stupid bitch, but she was a good mother to the boys. He had never treated her with respect so he understood her motive for divorcing him and not allowing the boys to visit him in prison, but he was determined not to lose the boys despite that, even though he had never really spent any time with them. His letters to them had come back "return to sender." He needed them to visit him in prison.

He could never seem to walk the straight and narrow path in life, and he didn't seem to feel the slightest bit of guilt or remorse about that. He was an enigma to himself. Still in time, he knew he could wile his sons into seeking a relationship with their "old man." He had plenty of time to think about his strategy.

CHAPTER 42

September 10

The next day had gone by and still no break in the case. Doug came home after having spent another full day perusing his case files. Reporters were lined up outside his house from the various local TV stations begging for an update or comment as to how the family was holding up. Doug referred them to the police for updates but paused long enough to thank them for their concern. The pain on his face revealed the answer to their question.

"The strain and stress on my family is almost more than we can bear, but like other families who have gone through similar experiences, we will get through this too. We appreciate all of our family and friends who have upheld us. Thank you." He smiled a feint smile and turned to walk into the house, making it clear the interview was over. The reporters seemed to respect his feelings. Doug's gentle and kind demeanor was so evident, reporters didn't have the heart to press him as they would others.

As he walked into the house, Snuggles was reposed by Paul on the family couch. Paul was just sitting there, looking straight ahead. He had been crying. His face was flushed and his eyes swollen. Doug studied him while he stood in the doorway.

"Are you all right, son?"

"Did I send Taylor to her death, Dad?"

"You both are adults, Paul. She made a choice just like you did. You both have led such sheltered lives and were naïve to how evil the world can be. It's a world I work in, Paul, but I never wanted you to become acquainted with that world. I may have brought that world home with me and jeopardized the safety of all of you." He sat down on the couch beside Paul and gave him a hug. Snuggles positioned his head on Paul's lap, seemingly to try to comfort him. Dogs had such a sense about them. Paul stroked Snuggles' head. The dog's large, bulging eyes never left Paul's face. He crawled up in Paul's face and began to lick his tears.

Snuggles was a caramel colored Lhasa Apso with black ears and a black tail. She was beloved by every member of the Conrad family, but Snuggles had always been Cynthia's dog. If only Snuggles could talk and tell what she saw that day Cynthia was snatched from the house.

Doug went upstairs to take a hot shower. When he stepped into the bedroom after his shower, Snuggles was lying across Cynthia's side of the bed, her head resting on Cynthia's pillow.

"Hey, Pooch! You miss your mommy like we do, don't you?" Doug picked up the dog and embraced her as he looked out the bedroom window from the second floor.

He drew Snuggles closer to him and whispered in her ear, *"We'll bring Mommy and Taylor home soon. I promise."* Snuggles laid her chin on his shoulder as if she understood while Doug's chin was quivering. Oh how he wished he could believe his own words.

CHAPTER 43

C ynthia waited for Quinton to enter the shed but he didn't. She remained breathless, fearing these may be her last minutes of life.

Brady Randolph had hunted white-tail deer in these woods for thirty years. As he walked deeper into the woods, he reminisced about the fun times he had had hunting with his dad and brother here. Both of them were dead now, and it brought a deep sadness to his heart. The old deer blind had served them well for the past fifteen years. Brady had been a craftsman in carpentry and had built their deer blind to last far beyond their hunting days.

He had taken a day's vacation to enjoy solitude in the woods and try out his new bow as he hunted for an antlerless deer for this time of year. He had always abided by Prince William County laws and followed all hunting regulations. He had convinced himself that today was his lucky day and that he would be bringing home venison to his wife. The grandkids loved to spend the weekends with Papa and eat *reindeer burgers*.

He had been sitting quietly in the deer blind for hours and hadn't seen one deer yet nor had he heard any movement. Few people knew of this isolated area, but it had a high deer population. He opened his thermos and drank some coffee and decided to eat his brown bagged lunch. He had packed two bologna sandwiches and a banana. He had brought two green apples with him. One for a snack and one to throw out to lure a deer. Having completed his sandwiches, Brady threw the Hefty one zip sandwich bag over the top of the deer blind in order to keep his area clean. It was less junk to rattle or to carry back to the car, plus he hoped he would be dragging a deer with him.

Several hours later as it was nearing dusk, Brady heard movement. He knew immediately what it was; a second later he spotted the deer and slowly readied his bow. It walked calmly yet quietly through the trees totally unaware of Brady's presence and oblivious to any impending danger.

Brady could feel the adrenaline rush begin. He had shot dozens of deer over the years, but every time he was ready to kill, he experienced the adrenaline shakes. He was a gentle man who loved and respected nature, but he knew that the deer population had to be thinned for their own good. He never killed an animal that he hadn't intended on eating, so he wasn't feeling guilty. It was just that to kill anything was a bit of a shock psychologically. It would soon pass.

He could hear the deer snort a little and look around cautiously. It was, oh, so close to the green apple on the ground—approximately twenty-five feet away from him. The deer took several more steps over to where the apple was and bent down to claim its prize.

Brady had a broadside shot at the doe. He aimed for the heart just behind the shoulder blade. Pulling the bow back, he released the arrow. The quiver passed through the lung and was a quick, clean, ethical kill. The deer was able to upright itself and took several steps forward before collapsing.

Brady quickly descended the deer stand and rushed to the doe, thankful he wouldn't have to track the dying deer through the dense woods. It was a large doe and she weighed approximately 250 lbs. by his estimation. He guessed the doe to be eight or nine years old. She was about six feet long and had stood three to four feet high. He and Glenna would be enjoying a lot of venison for the next year, that was for sure. As soon as he got home, he would call the grandkids over to see the deer before he dropped it off to the meat store.

He put on his gutting gloves and removed his heart and liver bag, one large absorbent dry towel, one sanitary wet towel, and one litter bag as he was getting ready to do the field dressing and tag the doe.

He propped the deer on its back and with his Browning drop point knife cut from just above the genitals up to her rib cage. He chose not to cut through a number of ribs as his dad preferred doing. He then turned the doe on her side and allowed the guts to fall out, cutting away the fat that held the intestines in. This was at the top of the cavity in the spine area. He was careful not to puncture the doe's bladder. With the guts half in and half out, he cut the diaphragm away from the deer's chest cavity and reached as far into its cavity as possible. Brady slid his sharp knife into the deer's chest and cut the esophagus, then simply pulled out the heart and lungs. With it came the rest of the intestines.

He did as much as he could with the deer while in the woods and washed up the best he could. Dragging the deer out of the woods by himself was going to be hard, but he would manage once he positioned the deer on his new Dead Sled Deer Drag. The problem would be hoisting the deer into the back of his truck all by himself.

His dad had passed away over two years ago. How his dad would have enjoyed being along today and sharing his kill. His brother died four months ago, and he would have shared the excitement of the moment as well. Had Drew been there, he would have helped him lug the doe to the truck. A sadness swept over him as he thought of his loss.

It had cooled down considerably, but Brady, nevertheless, was perspiring while dragging his prize doe through the dense woods. There was a rather narrow manmade path that deer hunters, no doubt, had made as they trudged through the woods looking for the perfect place to await a clear shot at a trophy deer.

As he was making his way back to his truck, he could hear the sound of a vehicle coming down the same dirt road as he had traveled to park his truck. The wood was so quiet and peaceful, any sound seemed to resound through the trees. He could barely see car lights shining through the trees. Instead of sensing danger, he was in great hope that it might be someone capable of helping him hoist his doe in the truck. This was such a desolate spot, Brady assumed the person would most likely be a hunter or poacher.

He continued pressing forward along the path dragging his doe with less than an eighth of a mile to go before he reached the truck.

Before Quinton got out of his car, he saw the truck. He had no idea whose it was, but he certainly hadn't anticipated company here. This could foil his plans, and he couldn't afford that to happen. He put his window down to listen but heard nothing. He pulled out his gun, grabbed a small bag from off the car seat, and walked to the shed. The chick had better be there or his life could be changed forever. He wasn't going down alone if things went wrong. He would have to call in the "*higher powers to be*" for better cover and more money for his silence.

Cynthia heard the car door slam and stood along the wall in the corner. She was baffled by all the different doors slamming at different times and yet no one entered the shed. She knew she couldn't go much longer without food and especially water, and even though she was feeling weak, she refused to cower or appear afraid, even though she was terrified each time Quinton entered the shed. She knew he had a definite plan for her and in a time frame, but the specific plans were nebulous.

Quinton looked all around and seeing no one, unlocked the door.

"So what's goin' on, Cindy?"

"Please. I need food and water. I also need to go to the bathroom."

"Well, Mr. Nice Guy here brought you a nice big bottle of H_2O and a banana. You look like the type who eats healthy and watches her figure. So, it looks like we've had a visitor. Anybody we know?"

Quinton studied her face to assess her reaction to the truck's owner. She showed no signs of knowing what he was talking about.

"Have you been talking to anyone, Cynthia?"

"No. I don't know what you're talking about. How could I know if someone's around. There aren't any windows, so I can't see out."

Of course, she had heard a car slam hours and hours before, but she assumed it was Quinton. When he didn't enter the shed, she wasn't sure what was going on.

He put the small sack on the floor.

"For you, Cindy, but if I hear a peep out of you in the next half hour, I will kill you and this will be your last meal. Understand?"

"Ye, but I need to go the bathroom really bad."

"I'll be back very soon. Not a sound." He put his right index finger to his lips as if to say, Shhh.

He left the shed and locked it back. Without hesitation, she opened the sack and drank the water until it was almost gone. She savored every bite of the banana. She had always liked bananas, but this one tasted so good. Of course, she knew it was because she was so hungry, but the fact that he even brought her something to sustain her life seemed like it was a hopeful sign. She would try to flatter him so he would bring her more food. If she could win his trust, maybe she could find an opportunity to escape.

Earlier she had discovered a miniature golf score sheet and a small pencil in her pants pocket. She and Paul had gone to Rolling Greens Miniature Golf Course one evening several weeks back and played putt putt. The two of them had always enjoyed that activity together. They were quite competitive with each other now that Paul was grown, but they mostly enjoyed the camaraderie.

She had played it out in her mind that if she had to fight for her life, the pencil, as small as it was, would have to serve as the only weapon available to her. Obviously Quinton wasn't after their money or possessions. His crime seemed to be one of revenge, so he was after *blood*, starting with hers, so it seemed. Her strength was no match for his, but if she were able to incapacitate him, she would have a chance of escape. Poking him in the eye with the pencil, hitting him in the solar plexus with her elbows, and a swift kick to his groin—as an element of surprise—could give her time to escape if given an opportune moment. She had learned these things in her self defense class years ago, never dreaming in her wildest imagination, that she might have to put these skills to use. She would try to avoid all of the human contact if she could—just running away would be her ideal situation. She felt confident as a faithful jogger that she could outrun Quinton.

CHAPTER 44

Brady was nearing the break in the woods where it became less dense and he had parked his red Ford truck. He was glad because he was tiring. He surely hoped there was someone nearby he could ask for help.

Quinton looked around. He walked to the Ford truck and looked in it. The doors were locked but the bed of the truck had a plastic tarp in it. More than likely the owner was deer hunting and should be calling it quits soon. But how could he be sure Cynthia hadn't yelled out to him, and he called for help on a cell phone. Police could be on their way by now. He needed to find this man and in moments of talking to him would know if he knew . . .

Quinton then spotted the guy breaking through the brush, dragging a huge doe along the narrow, rugged path.

"Need some help, mister?"

"You bet! I was wondering how I was going to get this big girl in my truck all by myself. I could sure use your help."

Quinton saw that his bow was secured in its Primo's soft bow case. He knew the hunter would also be carrying a filet knife, but that would be no match for his four inch barrel Taurus Judge revolver.

"Been hunting here long?"

"Before sunrise. I've been coming here for about thirty years or more. Used to come here with my dad and brother."

110

"Oh yeah. Are they here with you?"

"No. Both died, so I'm hunting alone. Sure do miss them."

Cynthia could hear Quinton talking to someone—could even hear parts of the conversation. She knew the guy was a deer hunter, and that meant he would have a weapon, most likely a rifle. Doug had never been a hunter, so she never really knew much about it. It didn't seem like it was time for deer season in Akron. Was it possible she was in another state? Perhaps Pennsylvania or West Virginia? That would mean Quinton had violated a federal law in her abduction, and that the F.B.I. could be involved in the search for her.

She knew if she didn't scream out for help now, she may never be found nor rescued. It might be her one and only chance for survival. Indecisiveness could cost her her life; however, by doing so, she could jeopardize another person's life. There was simply no time to vacillate. As she whispered a prayer to God for help, she heard the men count to three and then heard what most likely was the deer hitting the truck bed or trunk.

"Help me, please!" she screamed. *"I'm Cynthia Conrad, and I've been kidnapped!"*

Brady froze as he heard her screams. He heard every word. A look of confusion came over his face.

"What's going on? That's coming from the shed."

"Right you are, old buddy!"

Brady had a look of fear on his face as he reached for the knife out of its sheath. He immediately sensed danger and could see an almost demonic look on the nameless man's face. Before he could process it all, Quinton pulled out his revolver and shot the hunter once at close range with one 45 long colt bullet. That left him with four more bullets. Brady fell face down at the rear of his truck.

As soon as Cynthia heard the gunfire, she froze with fear. She stood in total silence, hoping that the good guy was left standing. Then she heard Quinton's voice.

"Well, bitch, you just got an innocent guy killed. Hope you're happy now!"

Cynthia began to sob and slid down the wall, cowering in the corner. *"Oh, God, no, no . . . please say he didn't kill him. Forgive me, oh God, please forgive me . . . what have I done?"*

Quinton knew all along he was going to have to kill the guy. He couldn't take a chance that the guy would get suspicious as to what he was doing out there at dusk and start snooping. If the hunter had heard noises coming from the shed when he arrived, he would have freed Cynthia and called the police earlier. Well, he got lucky there!

So Quinton was sure the hunter knew nothing about what was going on. Poor chap walked into the wrong place at the wrong time. As many crimes as Quinton had committed over his lifetime, murder was not something he had ever planned to do. He knew he was on the brink of committing four more murders anyway, but after his first time it really wasn't as hard as he thought it would be. The first two kills were for self preservation, but the next four would be murders of revenge, for sure. This killing, however, could complicate everything, for now the hunter's family would report him missing. If the family knew where he went hunting specifically, they would send authorities out to look for him or come out to check for themselves. This was messing up everything, for now he would have to either kill Cynthia immediately or move her location, which would be risky.

Quinton removed the hunter's wallet and shuffled through it. Brady Randolph, 60 years old. Quinton removed the $37 from his wallet.

"That will come in handy, Brady. After all, you certainly won't need it. Wish it had been a lot more, though."

Quinton checked his jacket pocket and removed his truck keys. He unlocked the truck and opened the glove compartment. He found another twenty dollars and a few restaurant gift cards. Another gift from old Brady! He confiscated everything useful to him and then walked back to Brady's body.

He needed to make a phone call to his son. Kevin needed to bring the daughter to him immediately. He should be on his way, but time was crucial now.

If he could make it appear that the hunter killed Cynthia and then killed himself, that would be awesome. He wasn't sure he could pull that off.

He checked every pocket on Brady once again and searched his truck thoroughly looking for a cell phone. Fortunately, he didn't have one. Brady was an old fashioned guy, and that was good. Brady's family wouldn't be calling him to see where he was or why he wasn't coming home. More than likely, neither his wife, mother, nor sister-in-law ever knew their exact hunting location; but Quinton didn't feel comfortable risking that. He was going to have to make a decision pretty fast about what to do with Cynthia and then Taylor when she arrived. The two Conrad girls were easy to abduct, but the son and father would be much more challenging. They would come later.

CHAPTER 45

Quinton called Kevin on his cell phone.

"Kevin, where are you?"

"I'm crossing into West Virginia now, Dad. I'm assuming from what you told me, I'm less than an hour's drive away from you."

"That should be right. You have the directions once you get to the dirt road, right?"

"Yeah, Dad."

"You have the girl, right?"

"Yeah, I have her in the trunk, but I wasn't sure how much chloroform to put on the rag. I was afraid I'd give her too much and kill her, but I'm afraid she might awaken and start screaming for help or banging on the trunk lid. She's going to be okay, isn't she, Dad?"

"Sure, son. As I told you, I'm just detaining them as a distraction for someone whose very important and very rich in Akron. I'm getting paid very well for doing this. And then when I'm told it's safe to release them and I get my money, I will let them go safe and sound."

"I want a new life, Kevin. I've made lots of mistakes in my life. I know I've screwed up. Few people will give an ex-con a fair chance at a job, so this is my one opportunity to make some fast money—where no one gets hurt—and start life all over. Your mom divorced me, and I at least want to make it all up to you. Maybe in time I can win your

brothers over, and we can have the father-son relationship we all want. That is what you want, isn't it, son?"

"Yes, Dad, it is."

"Good. So get the girl here safely. Remember, as soon as you pass her over to me, I want you to leave so you don't get mixed up in this. When the air is clear and I get the money, I'll call you and we'll head for Las Vegas. Gambling, partying, and girls! Until then, stay focused, son."

"I will, Dad, but I'll be glad when this is over."

"Me too, son. Like I said, stay focused and keep your mouth shut."

"Okay, Dad."

CHAPTER 46

Kevin drove another two miles until he came to a long driveway that led to a farmhouse that seemed vacant. He was feeling uneasy about this entire thing, but he needed to stretch and wanted to check on Taylor. He stepped out of his car and walked to the trunk and opened it. Even though the trunk lid light was dim, he could see that Taylor was awakening and her eyes showed fear. Very softly he spoke.

"Taylor, you're going to be all right. I promise. I'm taking you to see your mother. Once you're reunited with her, you'll feel better. She's safe and you will be too. It won't be much longer and you will be back home safely, so, please, cooperate with me. Okay?"

She nodded her head. Her mouth had been taped shut, so she could only make sounds.

"I'm sorry, Taylor. You just don't understand."

He shut the trunk lid down as gently as he could and got back into the car. He put the car in reverse until he could point the car to the main road heading southeast. Few cars were on the road this late at night, so he turned the light on and reviewed his dad's directions one more time. He had it memorized, but the closer he got, the more nervous he became. As he got older, his mother would, on a rare occasion, share a story about their father that made him appear so mean, but now that he met his dad a month ago at an out of the way truck diner, he could tell that prison life had changed him and he truly wanted to make things up to him and his brothers. Kalen and Kerry showed no interest in reuniting with their dad, but he did. It was something he had always wanted, and he wasn't going to be denied now. In fact, prior to their recent meeting, he hadn't seen his dad since he was probably four years old. He couldn't even remember what he looked like had it not been for a few family pictures that he had of his dad. Mom had divorced Dad as soon as he went to prison and would never allow any of them to visit him in prison.

Mom had always been honest with them about why their dad was in prison, so he knew that his dad had killed a clerk in the process of a robbery. Mom did believe their dad when he said he hadn't meant to kill the man, that he had merely panicked, but the man was dead, nevertheless. She admitted that Dad had a violent side to him and that she had feared him during much of their marriage. While he had been belligerent with her, he had really never mistreated the boys. Dad had lots of time to think about what he had done with his life while in prison. He had regrets, and a man had a right to be forgiven once he paid his due to society, didn't he? Being a little older, Kalen and Kerry had more memories of their father, but he still thought in time, they would seek a relationship with Dad. Well, he wanted to help his dad get back on his feet and at least give their relationship a chance.

CHAPTER 47

Kerry Reed had just stepped inside his apartment after a hard day's work. He had been an auto mechanic with a Buick dealership three miles from his apartment for the past three years. He quickly stripped down, throwing his uniform on the bathroom floor, and took a hot shower. He always felt grimy after leaving the shop and the hot shower was a way not only to clean up but to relax his sore muscles. He loved his job but it was more physical than most people thought. Fortunately, hc was healthy and could easily lean into the engine for hours without any pain or discomfort. He enjoyed the challenge of diagnosing car problems, so his job was never boring. But when his eight hour shift was over, he was ready to call it quits.

With a towel wrapped around his waist, he walked into his bedroom, flipped on the TV and walked over to his closet to select his clothes for meeting his buddies at Jerzees, a sports bar, to watch Monday night football.

The Channel 3 news was on and Kerry's attention was captured suddenly.

"Cynthia and Taylor Conrad's disappearance are still a mystery, but Taylor was believed to have been meeting a male friend named Tim Smith. However, the police now believe the male's name is not Tim Smith at all but rather an alias. He had falsely identified himself not only to Taylor but to her entire family a week back at a cookout at their house.

He is now a "person of interest" in Taylor's disappearance and the police ask that if anyone knows who this young man may be, he is to call Sgt. Dennis Parker at 330-375-0472. Kerry looked up and saw a picture of Kevin, his brother. He couldn't believe what he was seeing. *" This is Erin Wright reporting for Channel 3 News."*

Kerry picked up his phone and called Kevin's cell phone number. He apparently didn't have it on. Kerry then called his mother.

"Mom, have you been watching the news tonight?" He sounded alarmed to Ramona.

"No, I haven't. What's up, son?"

"I'm not sure, but Kevin's picture was flashed on the screen as a person of interest in the disappearance of Taylor Conrad, the daughter of that lady who has been missing for several days."

"What? Surely you have to be mistaken, Kerry."

"I'm almost positive, Mom. I tried to call Kevin on his cell, but he didn't have it on. Erin Wright asked anyone who could identify the picture to call the police. There will be plenty of people watching the news who will recognize Kevin."

"How would Kevin even know this girl?"

"I don't know, Mom, but that was clearly his picture, even though it was not a really clear picture of him."

"I'll call you back in a few minutes, Kerry. I will make some calls."

Ramona paused for a moment, trying to process this news. She immediately tried to turn to different stations to get the news, hoping the story would be covered again on another station. Meanwhile, she tried calling Kevin on his phone and confirmed what Kerry had told her. Kevin didn't have his cell phone on. That in itself was odd. He was always available via the cell.

Ramona called several of Kevin's male friends to see if they knew where he might be right then. They didn't. He did tell them he was going away for a few days but didn't say where.

Ramona went to his bedroom as he still lived with her. He didn't spend any time at the house except to sleep, however. She began to look through everything. There was no note. Nothing seemed different or out of the ordinary. His bed had been left unmade, but he rarely made his bed. She couldn't tell if any of his clothes were missing.

Then calls starting coming in—from her father, other relatives, and neighbors who had seen the news story and Kevin's picture. There was no doubt she would have to call the police, but she needed to see the news story first. She just couldn't believe that her sweet Kevin could be involved in any such thing of this magnitude. There had to be an explanation for it. She flipped from news station to news station until one was in the middle of the Conrad disappearance case. Kevin's picture flashed up as only a *person of interest* in Taylor Conrad's disappearance, but the innuendo was if he knew something about Taylor's disappearance, might he know where Cynthia Conrad is also?

Ramona made the call to the Akron Police Department and asked for Sgt. Parker.

As soon as Sgt. Parker answered, Ramona tried to calmly reply:

"My name is Ramona Reed and I believe the young man you are looking for in the disappearance of Taylor Conrad may be my son, Kevin Reed."

Sgt. Parker got Ramona's address and told her he and Officer Preston would be at her home in about 15 minutes. She was not to talk to anyone in the meantime—not the press, not anyone unless it was Kevin, and she should ask him to turn himself in.

Almost as soon as Ramona hung the phone up, Kalen and Kerry arrived at her house. All were concerned for Kevin and a bit mortified at the circumstances their family was placed in. However, they had so many questions, but none of them knew what was going on.

Sgt. Parker and Officer Preston arrived in about twenty minutes and after the initial introduction, were escorted into the living room, where Ramona introduced them to both Kalen and Kerry.

Officer Preston showed Ramona and the brothers a picture used on the evening news. They all confirmed that the picture was indeed Kevin Reed. Now that they had a positive identification of their prime suspect,

Office Preston stepped out onto the porch and quickly obtained from the Ohio Bureau of Motor Vehicles the car model, color, and license plate number for Kevin's vehicle and put an all alert out for him throughout the state. He also ordered the department to run a criminal check on Kevin and get back to him.

Sgt. Parker told Ramona they would need to ask her some questions but assured her that Kevin was not in any trouble as far as they knew. They simply needed to ask him some questions. Ramona knew enough about the law to know he was most likely a *prime* suspect in this case, but she knew the police would be wrong. Kevin couldn't do any such thing.

"Do you know Taylor Conrad?"

"No."

"Do you know Cynthia Conrad?"

"No."

"Are you familiar with this case?"

"Certainly. It has been big news for the last several days."

"Do you know Doug Conrad?"

"Slightly." said Ramona.

Officer Preston looked up immediately as did Sgt. Parker.

"How, Mrs. Reed?"

"Mr. Conrad was the investigator that found the facts needed to convict my husband—my ex-husband, I mean, of a crime that sent him to prison for 15 years to life."

"What is your ex-husband's name and where is he now?"

"His name is Quinton Reed, and as far as I know, he's still in prison."

"Which prison?"

"Lorain Correctional Institution in Grafton, Ohio."

Ramona then detailed Quinton's crime for them.

Officer Preston once again rose from his chair and stepped out of the house. Once again he called the station and asked them to find out the prison status of Quinton Reed ASAP. They were to call back with an answer as soon as they found out.

Officer Preston then called Doug Conrad.

"Doug, we may have a break in the case. Do you recall a case where you sent a Quinton Reed to prison for killing a clerk at a 7 Eleven?"

"No. Why? "

" We may have found a link. Look up your records and get back to us as soon as possible. We need to know the details."

Doug Conrad hung up and told his son to come with him to the office.

"Who was that, Dad? What's going on?" He saw a look of hope on his Dad's face that he hadn't seen in three days.

"I need to look up a case that may be the break we're looking for, son."

Doug called Mitch to pull the Reed file only to find out that it was already on Mitch's desk and, coincidentally, he had just started a follow-up on it.

While continuing his interrogation of Ramona Reed, Sgt. Parker's cell phone rang.

"Yes?"

" Records show that Quinton Reed was released a month ago. He obtained an early release at Mayor Stanwick's request."

"Do we know why?"

"No. Just that it was granted."

"Mrs. Reed, did you know that your ex-husband was released from Lorain Correctional Institution over a month ago?"

"No." Ramona and both sons looked so shocked that Sgt. Parker was sure they were telling the truth.

"Have any of you seen him since his release or heard from him?"

"No" was their answer simultaneously.

"Did Kevin have any contact with his dad during his prison stay?"

"Not that I know of. If he did, he never said anything." Ramona's heart sank as she envisioned Kevin getting tangled up with Quinton. Emotions started welling up within her as she feared for Kevin.

"Do you have some updated pictures of Kevin, Mrs. Reed? We'd like to take those with us if we could."

Ramona went over to the mantel and took down Kevin's 8x10 senior picture and a few 4x6 pictures of him in his football and baseball uniforms she had taken before some of his games.

"Are you employed, Mrs. Reed?"

"Yes, I had no choice once my husband was sent to prison. I had to raise our three boys all by myself. It hasn't been easy, but all three of my sons have grown up to be fine boys. I don't believe Kevin could possibly be mixed up in this case."

"Where do you work?"

"I work for Dunford, Ruhlin, and Rucker law firm."

Something in that answer resonated with Sgt. Parker, but he couldn't put his finger on it.

"Can you think of any reason why Mayor Stanwick would ask for an early release for your ex-husband?"

"None whatsoever. I could ask Allen Stanwick, his nephew. He works for our law firm."

"Allen Stanwick works for your law firm? Allen who is a suspect in the murders of Mrs. McGrary and Madeline Stover?"

"Yes, I suppose he is a person of interest, as you say, but Mr. Stanwick has not been charged with that crime nor has their been any proof that he committed those crimes. I don't see what that has to do with Kevin. Mr. Stanwick has never met Kevin nor Quinton."

Ramona could see Sgt. Parker's mind racing. Even she could sense there might be some connection between these cases, although she couldn't process all of this information so quickly. Sgt. Parker, not wanting to draw attention to those leads, moved on in his questioning. This time he addressed his question to Kalen and Kerry.

"Did Kevin talk to you about your dad recently?"

"No, but he had shown an interest in getting back together with Dad when he got out of prison. He asked us if we wanted to meet Dad and reclaim a relationship. Neither of us did, and Kevin just dropped it. We figured it was a moot point since Dad was in prison and we didn't think he would be getting out for a long, long time."

"Why do you think Kevin wanted to meet your dad?"

"Well, he was so young when Dad went to prison, he really didn't know him all that well. He probably was curious about his own identity. Who doesn't want to know their dad? Even adopted kids search for their parents. There are questions you have for them. We never sensed that Kevin had such a deep yearning."

"To your knowledge, did Kevin ever visit your dad in prison?"

"No, I'm sure not," said Kalen.

"Did he ever write your dad or communicate by phone?"

"Not that I know of," said Kerry. Ramona confirmed that same belief.

Ramona and the two sons were asked to come to the station to make some formal statements and to be further questioned. They agreed to it, knowing they didn't have a choice anyway.

Ramona quickly asked Sgt. Parker. *"We don't know with certainty that my son is involved with Taylor Conrad's disappearance, do we?"*

"No."

"I don't want anyone hurting my son, and right now I fear for his safety."

"We just need to ask him some questions, Mrs. Reed. The sooner we can find him, however, the sooner we can eliminate him as a person of interest."

Ramona needed to go into her bedroom to get her sweater and her purse. While in there, she called Kevin's cell phone again. This time, it rang but he didn't pick up. Ramona left a message.

"Kevin, you need to call me right away. I need to know where you are. I'm concerned. I love you, son, and know you will always do the right thing."

CHAPTER 48

As soon as the mayor's office opened the next morning, Sgt. Parker and Officer Preston stepped into the posh office. The attractive middle aged secretary greeted them with a smile. The mayor had a very busy schedule, but she was trained to know that uniformed officers from the Akron Detective Bureau would surely take precedence. She called into Mayor Stanwick's office to inform him that Sgt. Parker and Officer Preston were here to see him for a few minutes. The mayor wasn't surprised to know this investigation had led to him since the case had escalated on the news. He paused for just a moment and then told his secretary to escort them in.

"Good morning, Mayor."

"Good morning, Officers. What can I do for you this morning?"

"We are working on the Conrad case and would like to ask you a few questions."

"Well, I don't know much about the case except what I've been hearing on the news, but I will certainly do whatever I can to help you."

"It has come to our attention that you recently submitted a request for an early release of Quinton Reed. Is that true?"

"Yes, I did."

"May we ask you why?"

"My nephew works with a relative of Mr. Reed's. He felt sorry for her as she supports Mr. Reed's three children, and so he asked me if

I could request an early release from prison. I reviewed his records to learn he only had two more months left before he would have been paroled anyway, so I agreed to help. His record while in prison had been impeccable, so I didn't see how it could hurt."

"Which nephew asked you for this request, Mr. Stanwick?"

"My nephew, Allen."

"Is that Allen Stanwick who remains a person of interest in the McGrary and Stover murder case?"

"Yes. I'm not really sure he is still a suspect. There hasn't been a grain of proof that he had anything to do with it. I hope someone is working on this case so that my nephew can finally be vindicated of these suspicions, detective."

"Mayor, do you know Douglas Conrad?"

"I know of him although I've never really met him. I talked to him over the phone once, I believe."

"Could you tell us about that conversation."

"Well, as you already know, the McGrary and Stover murder case had gone cold. I had heard that Mrs. McGrary's niece had hired Mr. Conrad to work on the case or for a better word re-open it. The murder weapon had never been found, but my nephew did own a gun similar to the one used in the murders. Unfortunately for Allen, his gun had gotten stolen around the time of that crime. I spoke with Mr. Conrad and asked him to fly to Chicago to follow Allen's footsteps in search of his missing gun. I was willing to finance the trip. As a matter of record, you know that Allen's parents live in Chicago, and he needed to get away from the media and all of the hype to relax, so he went to visit them. If Mr. Conrad could find the gun and prove that it wasn't used in the crime, Allen could be publicly exonerated."

"Well, what if he had found the gun, and it was, in fact, the weapon used?"

"Then I expect forensics would do their job with fingerprints and find the shooter, whoever it might be.

"People get their guns stolen everyday, Sgt. It happened to my nephew who happens to have his CCW license, by the way. He decided

to take the gun with him while driving alone to Chicago to visit his folks. Not thinking, he left his car unlocked while gassing up and going inside to pay and then use the restroom. He believes it may have been stolen then or at one of the several rest areas he stopped at along the way. Granted, he should have been more careful, but what is done is done.

"So, as you see, I, Allen, and our entire family want that gun found so Allen can be proven innocent. This is all a matter of record." Steve Stanwick tried hard not to sound defensive.

"Are you familiar with the details of the Conrad case, Mayor?"

"Some. Through the police chief but mostly the press, I have stayed abreast of the case. How is that going?"

"We're following up on some leads, but we haven't found Conrad's wife nor daughter. Is there anything you can share about Doug Conrad that might help us in this case?"

"No, I'm afraid not, but I hope it gets solved quickly for their sake and so that Mr. Conrad can continue with the McGrary case and prove my nephew innocent."

"Sorry to have taken up your time, Mayor."

"No problem."

"Oh. Just one more question."

"Yes?"

"Have you met Quinton Reed since his release from Lorain?"

"No."

"Goodbye, Mayor."

As soon as Sgt .Parker and Officer Preston had left the outer office, Steve Stanwick called Allen on his prepaid cell phone.

CHAPTER 49

Allen Stanwick happened to be in his car heading for an appointment when his Uncle Steve called and told him about the police inquiries concerning Quinton Reed. After having just spoken to his uncle, Allen pulled into a strip mall parking lot and began to dial a number on his prepaid cell phone.

Quinton was hoisting Brady's lifeless body into the back of the truck when his cell phone rang. He dropped the body and answered the phone on the second ring.

"Do you have anything to do with the disappearance of Taylor Conrad?"

"Who?"

"Taylor Conrad. Cynthia's daughter. She's disappeared."

"Not a thing. I swear. I've been busy looking and diving for your gun," he answered sarcastically.

"Well, they claim she's disappeared too, and they think she may have been abducted by a young kid."

"Well, uh, that wouldn't be me, now, would it?"

"She's probably run off with a boyfriend."

"It had better be something like that, but if I find out you have double crossed me in any way, Quinton, you will find out real quickly that you were dealing with the wrong guy. Do we understand each other?"

"Nothing to worry about, boss. I'm just trying to make some money and start my life over." He thought to himself, *"And you have no idea who you're dealing with, Mr. Stanwick."*

"So why haven't you called me with news?"

"Been kinda busy."

"Did you find and destroy the gun?"

"Sure did."

"And?"

"Did exactly what you told me to do with it."

"Great."

"And Cynthia Conrad?"

"Safe and sound."

"Put her on the line and tell her to provide her name, her social security number, and her date of birth."

"You're kidding, right?"

"No. I won't be speaking. I just want to hear her voice, verify she is alive, and then you'll get your money at the designated drop off location. We can't have any paper trail."

"Yes, boss."

Quinton unlocked the shed and entered it. Cynthia looked terrified but he gave her specific instructions as to what to say. He put the phone to her ear as her hands were still tied behind her.

With hesitation, she spoke. *"My name is Cynthia Conrad. My social security number is 333-57-4388, and I was born August 14, 1969."* She didn't hear a thing at the other end. She wanted to scream for help but worried it would make her situation worse, if it could be worse, that is.

Allen was convinced she was alive.

Quinton stepped out of the shed, locking it back while returning to the conversation with Allen.

"Release her so she can be found fairly quickly and get lost for awhile. Hang low. Remember, no one is to get hurt."

"When I get the money, I will release her. Not before."

"The cash will be at the designated location in less than ten minutes."

Allen knew that the cash had been in a hidden, remote place for over a day. When he had last spoken to Quinton, he knew he would soon be able to retrieve his gun and destroy it. He definitely didn't want a face to face meeting with Reed to deliver the money. Too much was at stake to do that, but he still needed confirmation that their agreement had been fulfilled. The money could not be traced to him or Uncle Steve and he used gloves when handling the bag. He had hidden it there at night, having worn dark clothes. He was sure no one had seen him. There could be no mistakes. His career and that of Uncle Steve's depended upon that.

His one fear was that Quinton would either try to blackmail him for more money or pretend he didn't get the money. He began to second guess whether he should have had Quinton return his gun to him so that he could destroy it himself and hide it, but he was never a good liar if questioned on the whereabouts of the gun under oath. And if he was questioned about it with the lie detector, it would clearly prove he was lying. This way, he could honestly say he didn't know where it was.

What he had on Quinton could send him away for life, so he doubted Quinton would betray him. By the same token, Quinton knew just enough about the gun to do more than arouse suspicions regarding him.

Allen would be glad when this ordeal was behind him. As soon as Quinton got his money and Cynthia Conrad was released, his problems would be solved. However, he couldn't help but feel uncomfortable about the missing daughter. He had nothing to do with that, but the coincidence was uncanny. Hopefully, she ran off with a boyfriend and will return home when she hears her mother has been found alive. Still, in his heart, he felt something was terribly wrong.

CHAPTER 50

Quinton knew he should quickly dispose of Brady's body, but getting the money was more important. He would retrieve the money and then return and do the clean up. Soon after, Kevin would be arriving with "the girl." After tonight, he could relax for awhile . . . before Part II of his plan. Paul and Doug Conrad would eventually let their guard down, and when they did, he would be there.

Quinton figured he would go have a late beer with Kevin at the Sudsy Tavern four miles down the way and then send him on home, promising, of course, to reunite with him soon.

Quinton got in his Taurus and made his way up the dirt path to the paved road. He turned east and drove approximately two miles to the designated location. It was dark but he managed to find the small pullover. There was almost no traffic on the road. There were only about two or three rundown farmhouses on this stretch of the road.

He looked in all directions before getting out of his car. He checked the gun in his pocket just in case he was walking into a trap. He walked into the woods and heard a trickling brook. He followed it for about 100 feet or so and saw a small orange rag tied to a white birch tree. He then spotted a camouflaged bag hidden under a bush next to the tall birch.

Quinton snatched the bag up and peeked in it to be certain it contained the money. He smiled. Not taking any chances of being double crossed, he quickly returned to the car, put his dimmer light on and counted the money. Fifty thousand dollars in packs of $100 bills were there. Not bad earnings for burning some clothes and finding a gun and chiseling off the serial number, especially when you were told approximately where to find the gun.

Quinton's quest for revenge was playing out better than he ever imagined. He couldn't believe he had help from a mayor and a lawyer. He had lots of protection from those in high authority should something go wrong.

For the first time in his life, Quinton had money and freedom. The only thing he needed now was some more booze and a woman. He had already chugged down two beers a few hours ago, so the booze could wait, but there was no reason anymore to show restraint with Cynthia. It had been a long time since he had been with a woman, and he was a hungry man. By the time he ravaged Cindy, it would be time to have a little fun with a young, wild thing. He aimed the Ford Taurus toward the shed.

CHAPTER 51

At least for now Quinton decided to throw Brady in the back of his truck and throw a tarp on top of him to conceal the body. Quinton looked around and enjoyed the stillness of the night. He put his gun under the driver's seat of his car before locking it and then hid both his car keys and the truck keys under Brady's body. He unlocked the shed, and hid the shed key under a large rock near the shed.

Quinton had his flashlight and walked in to the shed. Cynthia had heard the car door slam and was standing in the corner. As soon as she saw Quinton she begged him to let her go to the bathroom. Again, he made her take off her shoes and then he walked her over to the trees. As he slipped her sweats down, he continued staring at her. She quickly surveyed the area all around her, noticing the car and now a truck, but she didn't see a dead body lying anywhere. She was convinced he had killed someone, so she knew he was capable of killing again, and she was pretty sure who his next victim was going to be. She had previously seen the dirt road but just now had spotted the hiking path. Cynthia sensed that whatever his plan was for her was probably now moving to the next or final phase.

When she stood up he pulled up her sweats, he grabbed her clothing from behind and led her back to the shed. He turned on his flashlight and shut the shed door. She didn't like the look on his face. He started to come near her and basically she backed herself in the corner. He untied her arms and legs.

"Now for some fun, Cynthia." He had his arms around her and she could feel his hardened body up against her. She smelled beer on his breath, but he didn't appear inebriated. He began to unzip his jeans while fondling her breasts. She was in trouble. Her courage disintegrated immediately and she began to cry.

"Please. Please, don't!" she cried. *"I have been faithful to my husband for 25 years."*

"Listen, bitch! My goal is to hurt your husband in the biggest way possible. Like he hurt me. He took away my freedom, my life, my family, and he's going to see what that feels like just before he dies."

"But you haven't hurt me. You could walk away right now and . . ."

Quinton forcefully removed her top and pulled her sweats down. He was overpowering. She began to panic and decided now was the time to fight him with all of her strength and might.

Quinton grabbed her hair and pulled her head back. He tried to kiss her and press himself on her. She scratched his face and angrily he grabbed her arms and threw her across the shed to the other side of the wall. She was crying and half dazed by the force of the shove.

"I have nothing to lose now. My future is totally doomed, but I will never go back to prison. Never.

"Listen, Cindy, Taylor will be here in just a short while and when she comes, I will just have practiced on you. I will teach Taylor everything she wanted to know about men and enjoy her young, tender body."

"No! Don't you dare touch her! Please, do whatever you need to do to me, but leave her alone. I beg of you. I will do whatever you want. Just leave her alone."

"Fine."

Cynthia was frozen with fear. She had to get out of this shed alive and get help. That was her only hope of saving Taylor. Quinton was showing what his capabilities were, and she was totally frightened of this man. He was dangerous.

Cynthia slunk to the floor in submission to Quinton. His appetites were voracious and there was no end to his desires. He was rapacious. After it was all over, she figured he would probably try to kill her. To her shock, he held on to her and shortly thereafter, his breathing slowed and she heard him snoring. Could it be? Was he really sleeping or was he trying to trick her? She waited for awhile until she was convinced he was in a pretty good sleep state. She moved his arm and got up and grabbed her clothes and shoes. She quietly opened the shed door and closed it. She tried to open the car but it was locked. She tried the truck next but it, too, was locked. She looked for keys as quickly as she could, but she figured he would have them hidden pretty well, and if she dallied, he could catch her again. She looked in the back of the truck and lifted the tarp. That's when she saw the dead man. She became almost hysterical but had no time to search his pockets. The best thing for her was to flee. She thought if she ran up the dirt road, he would get in his car and spot her with his headlights. It would be too easy to catch her. So she decided to run for the woods and follow the rugged path. Maybe it would connect with the dirt road eventually or lead out to somewhere. She went down the path for a certain length and quickly put her clothes and shoes back on . It would only be a matter of time and he would awaken and pursue her.

It was a full moon which lit up the woods fairly well. That was good for her, but that was also helpful to Quinton too. This was her moment of freedom and probably her only chance to survive.

She sprinted as fast as she could, knowing that Quinton could awaken any moment. If she fought her way through the trees and bushes, he could certainly hear and maybe even see the movement and know exactly where she was. She realized as she ran that she was short of breath and dehydrated. She felt weak partly from not eating nor drinking for days, and partly from the terror she was feeling. She would have to depend on her adrenaline rush. After all, she was fighting for her very life—her very survival and maybe that of Taylor's—so all thoughts had to be cast aside and she needed to focus solely on staying alive. All she had to do was outrun Quinton or hide so well he couldn't find her until she could find her way to the main road.

She continued to run with just enough light to see several feet in front of her. Shadows from giant firs tended to obliterate the path. She tripped on her shoestrings and fell forward, scratching her face and forearms. As she continued to run, some of the branches extended across the path, scratching her face or getting caught in her hair. The adrenaline rushing through her body voided out any pain, however. Never before had she found herself in such a life-threatening dilemma.

The path opened up wider and she spotted a deer blind in a tree. She could easily climb up there, but it would be too obvious of a hiding spot. Quinton would definitely stop to check that out. If she was up there, she'd have no way to escape. As she paused long enough to consider whether she should stay on the path or get off, she bent over to tie her shoestrings. That's when she spotted an empty sandwich bag on the ground. No doubt a hunter left it there while hunting. Cynthia decided to write a quick note per chance she didn't live through this ordeal. Perhaps someone would find it and eventually Quinton would get caught.

She removed the putt putt score sheet and the little score pencil out of her pocket and quickly penned a note:

Quinton white male 6' 2" brown eyes/hair. Arrest him. Goal to kill our entire family. Doug u will always be the love of my life. I owe u so much. Love our kids 4 me 2. Cynthia.

She closed it up in the zip lock bag and slipped it under a bush near the deer blind.

She took off again when she heard a sound not far behind her.

CHAPTER 52

Quinton awakened and saw that Cynthia was gone. The door was slightly ajar. He was furious. He had just made a HUGE mistake. He rushed out of the shed and looked around. The car and truck were still there so she was on foot. He put his jeans and boots on quickly, got in the car and pulled out his gun and grabbed the flashlight. He slammed the car door shut and quickly headed down the path in pursuit of Cynthia. She couldn't have gone that far. If she went up the road, it would be too easy to catch her. He was pretty sure she would take the path and go through the woods.

The full moon was going to be a good advantage for him. He stopped to listen and he heard rustling deep in the woods. Just then Quinton saw car lights coming down the dirt road. That had to be Kevin. He waited for the young man to pull up.

"Kevin! Stay here and keep the girl in the trunk for the time being. I've got a problem! I'll be back in a few minutes."

Kevin saw the gun in his father's hand and he was terrified.

"What's going on, Dad?"

"Just do as I say Kevin!" He didn't plan for this to happen when Kevin arrived.

Well, it was what it was. He ran down the narrow path and out of sight.

Kevin walked over to the truck. It was locked. He lifted up the tarp in the back and jumped back when he saw the dead man and a dead deer. He began to hyperventilate. He quickly cupped his hands over his nose and mouth and leaned up against the truck. Trying not to become hysterical, he decided to step inside the shed. He saw a man's shirt on the floor. Something told Kevin that things weren't quite the way his dad said they were. Who was this dead man? Did his dad kill him? Was his dad chasing Taylor's mom? He opened the Ford Taurus and saw a bag. He looked inside it and saw the money—lots of money. That part of his dad's story must be true. He didn't know what was happening now, but he didn't like the looks of it, and he sensed something bad was happening. What had he gotten himself into? He opened the trunk lid and sat Taylor up so she could breathe easier. Both her hands and feet were secured.

CHAPTER 53

Cynthia heard Quinton yell out to her.

"Cynthia, you shouldn't have run. We were getting along so well. Taylor is here, and I thought you'd like to see her before you both die."

Cynthia stopped at the sound of Taylor's name. What if he did have her? What if he planned to rape her? She had to make a lightning quick decision to go back for Taylor's sake or run for help. His having Taylor could be a bluff. She turned back around and continued sprinting down the path.

Quinton got a glimpse of her and with his sight aimed for the middle of her back. He fired the gun and Cynthia dropped. He walked over to her and was convinced she was dead. The Judge was a convincing weapon, and the laser made the target so easy.

"Well, one down, Dougie. Two more to go before I come after you."

Feeling no remorse, he headed back for the shed but worried about what he would tell Kevin. He didn't want to get Kevin involved in murder, but Kevin made his own decision to get involved, and Kevin's role in bringing Taylor to him made his plan so much more expedient.

CHAPTER 54

Kevin heard the gunfire, and although he wasn't sure what was going on, he had a pretty good idea who his dad was pursuing. If his dad did indeed kill this man in the back of the truck and maybe killed Taylor's mother, what was he going to do to Taylor? This wasn't at all the plan his dad had described to him. This was not what Kevin was all about. The plan seemed innocent, but this was serious stuff. Confused and frightened himself, Kevin made a decision to abort his dad's plan. He had seen enough for major concern. He quickly untied Taylor's hands and feet and lifted her out of the trunk She began to take off her mouth gag. Before she could say a word, he gave her quick instructions.

"Something has gone terribly wrong, Taylor. I don't know what's going on, but you need to take my car and get out of here now! Go up this dirt road until you come to the paved road. Turn left on it and get to the first farmhouse you can and have them call the police. Get them here as fast as you can! Don't stop for anyone or anything! Go!"

Without hesitation, Taylor did exactly what he said. She got behind the wheel of the car and drove up the dirt road as fast as she could. Her heart was beating so fast she thought she was going to have a heart attack. If only she had her cell phone with her, she could call her dad. He would know what to do. Both Dad and Paul were probably frantic.

She got to the paved road and turned left. It seemed like forever before she got to a farmhouse. There were no lights on at the house, but she ran to the porch and pounded on the door, screaming for help. In a few minutes, she saw a middle aged man appear at the door. He put the porch light on and spoke to her through the door.

"Who are you and what do you want?"

"Please call the police! I need help! Can you possibly let me in? I'm afraid someone is after me! My name is Taylor Conrad."

He refused to open the door. She identified herself once again, stated that she had been abducted, didn't know where she was, and needed protection.

"I'll call the police, Ma'm! Try to calm down."

The man relayed that information to the police, and they assured the man they would be at the house in about ten minutes. The man yelled out to Taylor stating she should wait in her car, keep the doors locked, and that the police would be there in ten minutes. His porch light went off. The man stepped away from the window but looked out through a curtain to assess the situation. Unsure of the circumstances and not sure that this girl was truly alone, he grabbed his loaded rifle for the ready.

CHAPTER 55

K evin stood at the entrance of the shed when he saw the man he believed to be his dad coming up the path. Kevin rushed to him.

"Dad, what's going on? Were you shooting someone? Who is the dead man in the back of the truck? Where is Taylor's mom?"

So Kevin saw too much and was putting things together much more quickly than he had anticipated. He also asked with an accusatory attitude, which he resented.

"Where is Taylor, Kevin?"

"I sent her away. I saw the gun . . . heard the gunfire in the woods . . . Nobody was supposed to get hurt. That's what you said."

"What do you mean you let her go?" Quinton feared his entire plan was unraveling.

"You are my father, Quinton, aren't you?"

"I don't have time for introductions, son. I need to know where this girl went. We've got to get her back. How could you betray your old man like that? We had a plan, an agreement. Now where did she go?"

"I don't know. I told her to get back to the main road and turn right."

"Get in the car with me. We're going to go find her. What kind of car were you driving?"

"What are you going to do with her, dad? What have you done to her mother?"

"Get in the car, Kevin!" he yelled angrily.

"No! Who is that dead man in the back of that truck? Did you kill him?"

"You ask too many questions. Let's get the girl and then I'll explain everything to you, son. I've got the money, and we can head out to Las Vegas and have us a good time!"

"I'm not going anywhere with you. I can't believe I trusted you!" Kevin lashed out. *"I'm calling the police."*

Just then, Quinton pulled out his Judge. *"You can't do that, son. I'm not going back to prison. I just needed a chance to make some money so I could get back on my feet and start life all over."*

Kevin saw the revolver pointed directly at him. Without a second thought, he turned and began zigzagging up the dirt road toward the paved road at full speed. The last thing he heard was a big blast and felt an impact as he fell face first into the dirt.

For the first time Quinton felt guilty. He was guilty of many bad things, but he never hurt his sons the way his dad had hurt him. He always felt that because of that, he was worth saving or *redeeming* as the prison chaplain told him once. He saw his son slumped into a pile, blood everywhere. He decided what was done was done, so he needed to find the girl before she could get to the police. He got into the Ford Taurus and gunned the engine as he bounced over the holes and large rocks on the dirt road. When he got to the paved road, he turned right, hoping his son had answered him honestly, but he had doubts. Quinton didn't know what model car his son was driving but it would have Ohio license plates. With a young girl driving alone, it should be easy to find her. If he didn't find her quickly, this dilemma could blow up in his face. With no further thought about Kevin, he gunned his motor in pursuit of Taylor Conrad.

CHAPTER 56

The county police arrived at the farmhouse and walked up to the car. Taylor immediately identified herself but was almost hysterical. The police asked her to step out of the car. She carried no identification on her so the police, explaining that this was normal procedure, they asked her to lean against the car while they searched her. They put her in the back of their squad car and one deputy searched the car she had been sitting in. She was sobbing, indicated concern for the safety of her mother and kept begging them to go back to the place she had just come from, yet she couldn't describe exactly where that was. To Taylor's shock, she was informed she was in West Virginia. The deputy had his office call the Akron Police Department to try and verify the girl's story and quickly were informed that an APB had been put out for Taylor Conrad and a young man named Kevin Reed; the young lady, however, kept referring to a young man by the name of Tim Smith.

Not sure exactly what was going on, the officer asked if Taylor could find the place where she had just been.

"I'm pretty sure I can, although it was dark."

They got back on the main road and went west until Taylor told them to slow down and stated there should be a dirt road close by. They spotted the road and turned down it. As they moved slowly down the dark road, their headlights caught a glimpse of a young man lying face down in the dirt. Unsure of what they might be walking into, one deputy radioed for backup.

"Oh my God! It's Tim. What's happened? He was alive when I left!"

It was then they were informed that they should be on the lookout for a possible felon named Quinton Reed who would more than likely be armed and dangerous. It was also possible he might have a woman named Cynthia Conrad with him who had been abducted from Ohio. They were reminded that this could be the famous case heard on ABC and NBC in the past few days.

Both police officers stepped out of the car with flashlights and weapons drawn. The one deputy knelt down by the boy's body and realized the young man was still alive. He was lying in a pool of blood unconscious but breathing. The one officer began applying pressure on the victim's wound to stop the bleeding. Taylor tried to get out of the car to help Tim but realized she was locked in. How could all this be happening to her and her family? What could the Conrads have possibly done to deserve all of this? Her head pressed against the window with tears streaming down her face. She studied the woods for any sighting of her mom.

"Please, Mom. Don't be in there. Please don't be in there."

Unsure how Tim was involved with the disappearance of her mother, she still prayed for his recovery as well as for her mom.

The other officer quickly returned to the car radio and asked for an ambulance ASAP! He then remained vigilant to their surroundings. He looked in the truck with his flashlight and saw nothing of concern. It appeared to be empty, so he then walked to the shed and looked in. It, too, was vacant. He then returned to the truck and looked in the bed, lifting up the canvas. It was then he saw the dead deer first but then a dead man somewhat concealed under the deer. He immediately told his partner. He then returned to the squad car and radioed in his findings and the need for the medical examiner. He provided the truck's license plate number to identify the owner of the truck. It came back immediately as Brady Randolph.

The officer returned to the young boy on the ground and relieved his partner, continuing to keep the pressure on the young boy. The officers could hear the sirens coming and knew that reinforcement was coming to help them. Hopefully, the paramedics could save him. The policeman returned to the car and asked Taylor if she had any idea who this young man was. She identified him as Tim Smith.

"Do you know a Kevin Reed, m'am?"

"No."

"Please. I need to call my Dad. Is there anyway I can call my family and let them know I'm okay?"

"We're going to get you back to the station, m'am, and piece this story together first and then we'll let you call your folks."

"But you don't understand. My mother could be out here in this woods fighting for her life. Her name is Cynthia Conrad. She's been missing since September 6th. My father is a private investigator and our family's safety has been in jeopardy ever since."

"We will do everything possible to reunite you with your family, m'am, but you will need to be patient. For your own safety, we need to get you out of here and back to the station. Besides, we can use your services in a greater way when we obtain more information from you. We won't leave here until we're sure your mother isn't here, so please try to calm down. We'll do everything we can to find your mom IF she is in our state."

Three squad cars arrived along with two F.B.I. agents and the EMS. The paramedics began working on the young man. They lifted him up on a gurney, placing an oxygen mask over his face. He was then hoisted into the ambulance. The doors were closed and Taylor only knew that Tim must at least still be alive.

After they had heard the sound of a gun firing, Tim had a change of heart and handed her the car keys and told her to get out of there quickly, stopping for nothing. When she had driven away, Tim was standing there very much alive, so he knew something. He knew they were not alone in those woods. Someone else was in those woods . . . someone with a gun.

CHAPTER 57

Quinton was speeding down the road when he heard the sirens coming. He saw several police cars speeding down the road with their lights flashing. He decreased his speed so as not to draw attention to himself as it appeared they were heading for a specific place. He wasn't sure if they were looking for him, going to the shed area, or were responding to the girl. Two police cars passed him by, oblivious to any passing cars, so he realized they weren't aware of who they should be looking for at this point. That meant for him there would have to be a change of plans. Besides, Kevin may have sent him on a wild goose chase.

If the girl was found, Doug Conrad would most likely come to West Virginia to pick her up and speak to the authorities as they were now involved in this case. But probably Paul Conrad would be left at home alone. Perhaps it was time to re-visit the Conrad house and take out Paul.

CHAPTER 58

As soon as the police car carrying Taylor had disappeared from the dirt road and was completely out of sight, the F.B.I. agents working with the local police department barked orders to every deputy present. With bullet proof vests on, flashlights lit, and guns drawn, they went in pairs to scour the area. One officer was instructed to stay with the truck, waiting for the forensics team to arrive.

As soon as Taylor got to the police station, she begged them to allow her to use a phone to call home. He asked her for the phone number and dialed it. No answer. She requested they try her Dad's cell phone number. Again, he dialed it for her. Doug Conrad picked up immediately.

"Mr. Conrad?"

"Yes."

"This is the Parkersburg County Police and we believe we have your daughter, sir. We're going to put her on the line."

"Thank God she's alive."

Taylor was almost hysterical.

"Dad, I'm in West Virginia. I was kidnapped by Tim. He drugged me and later told me he was taking me to see Mom. He put me in the trunk of his car."

"Slow down, Taylor. Are you all right?"

"Yes, but I'm scared. I'm scared for Mom. I don't know what's happening but something bad happened to Tim. He's been hurt, but if it wasn't for Tim, I might not be alive. I heard gun shots, Dad."

"Taylor, listen to me. His name isn't Tim. His name is Kevin Reed."

"Why would he lie to me . . . to us, Dad? What does he want from us?"

"Listen, Taylor, we're trying to piece all of this together. In order to find your mom, we need you to tell the police everything you know and can remember. Do you understand?"

"Yes, Dad."

"Now try to calm down. I need to talk to the police officer with you, and then I'm coming to Parkersburg to get you, Taylor. You will be safe now."

"Okay, Dad. Please hurry! Here's the officer."

Doug immediately identified himself and briefed the officer on the events of the past five days. He also let them know that his wife may be hidden nearby and that the police believe Kevin Reed may be the person who abducted Taylor. He also gave them Sgt. Dennis Parker's and Officer Preston's phone numbers who are the lead officers in this case.

CHAPTER 59

A report had come in from Brady Randolph's family concerned because he had not come home before nightfall, which was quite unlike him. They were sending a police officer to his home to fill out a missing person's report and obtain a picture of him, even if it appeared they had already found him. They wanted to tie together a time frame of Mr. Randolph's day before they broke the bad news to the family.

Both the West Virginia police and the F.B.I. agents had just heard of the Conrad case through the national TV stations but hadn't realized at first that they were being drawn into that very case. The Conrad family was just starting to gain national attention.

Doug Conrad had faxed Quinton Reed's file case to Officer Preston who then made a copy and faxed it to the authorities in Parkersburg, West Virginia. Doug quickly reviewed his notes and the old case was coming back to him. Doug sensed the feasibility of Quinton Reed being released from prison with a vendetta against him—like the one hinted in the note with Cynthia's underwear. If Quinton, a one time murderer and wife abuser had Cynthia, then Cynthia's life was in very real danger.

Doug immediately called Sgt. Parker and Officer Preston to verify they had received his fax when he learned they were boarding a helicopter to Parkersburg, West Virginia to aid in the investigation and bring Taylor back. Doug begged for them to allow him and Paul to ride along. They agreed, but Doug was instructed to keep away from the investigation and not interfere in any way.

In the helicopter, they could compare what each other knew. Any tidbit, no matter how insignificant it seemed, could be an important clue that could help them find Cynthia. So far they were lucky to find one Conrad alive unharmed. For Doug's sake, they hoped they could find Cynthia the same way. Somehow they knew that the next few hours could be the breaking point.

CHAPTER 60

F.B.I. agents Barry Brewster and his partner, Agent Patrick D'Andrea, took the foot path. They both looked through the woods to their left and right as well as straight ahead. Neither spoke but remained alert and attentive to any sound or movement. As they neared the homemade deer blind, they both halted.

It was possible that the perpetrator could be hiding in it or that Cynthia Conrad could be concealed there. No one yielded to their command to come down, so Agent Brewster covered Agent D'Andrea as he ascended the deer blind. It made for a very tense moment, not knowing if Quinton would be hiding there and begin shooting. Much to their relief, the deer blind was empty.

D'Andrea descended and they continued down the path. As they moved further, they saw a body lying face down, and it appeared to be that of a woman. Their hearts sank. They studied the environment around them and looked at their watch to determine the time. The woman had been shot in the back. They bent over and felt her cool body. Rigor mortis had not set in yet, but there was no question she was dead although they still felt for a pulse. This pretty much verified the girl's story.

They had no previous description of Cynthia Conrad except what they recalled from the newscasts, but what little they knew about this case, it appeared to be her. Their county had very few homicides per year, but tonight they had already discovered two with a possibility of a third if that young male didn't pull through.

Agent Brewster got on his cell and informed the coroner's office that there were now two dead bodies here in the woods and they were still searching the perimeter even further. They had to be careful not to compromise the crime scenes. After fifteen minutes continuing down the path, they decided to back track. They were looking for a weapon that may have been thrown in nearby bushes.

As they neared the deer blind again, the flashlight of Agent D'Andrea caught the tip of something shiny protruding from under a bush. He put his latex gloves on and picked it up. It was a sandwich bag. With a closer look, it appeared there was a note in it. It was in pencil but quite sloppy and very hard to read in the glare of the flashlight. They saw Cynthia's name at the bottom of the note and realized they had just found some important evidence. It looked like the mystery was coming to a sad conclusion for the Conrad family. At least his daughter had been found seemingly unharmed. Physically, that is.

After they read the note, both agents looked somber, shook their heads.

"She must have been a helluva woman and a perceptive one too! Cynthia, thanks to you, we will find this guy. You know what, Brewster? Some days I absolutely hate my job and today is one of those!" Agent Brewster agreed.

CHAPTER 61

While no one knew at this point what type of vehicle Quinton Reed was driving, they had already been sent an updated prison mug shot. They suspected he was driving a stolen car. An APB was put out for him.

Once the West Virginia authorities were brought up to speed in this case, they began to work together with the Ohio team to concoct a plan, promising to keep each other apprised of what was happening at both ends.

Doug and Paul Conrad with Officers Preston and Parker arrived at a small police station twenty miles outside of Parkersburg, West Virginia. Doug and Paul were informed of Taylor's emotional state. Doug and Paul were then permitted to see her. As soon as she saw them, she rushed into their arms, sobbing.

"Oh, Dad, I'm so sorry for disobeying you. I can't believe this is happening to us. What if Mom is . . . is . . . dead . . . What if she's out in the woods, Dad . . . I couldn't save her . . . I . . ."

Her legs completely went weak and came out from under her. She had been so overwhelmed and traumatized by the events of the last several hours, her body completely collapsed. Held up by her dad, Doug and Paul got her back in her chair. Smelling salts and a cool, wet cloth were administered to her quickly. As soon as she revived and was able to talk, she tried to tell her dad and Paul everything that had happened to her. She believed her mom was out there in those woods even though she never heard or saw her.

While Paul and Taylor seemed hopeful about the prospects of finding Cynthia safe, Doug was much more pessimistic but didn't say anything. As his heart raced inside his chest, he excused himself and walked over to Officers Preston and Parker. Preston was listening intently on the phone, and Doug studied his troubled countenance. Fear welled up in Doug and he sensed his worst fear may have become reality. Officer Preston hung up from his conversation.

"Doug, you need to stay here with your kids while we go investigate the location where Taylor had been taken."

"Have they found Cynthia?"

"You need to stay hopeful, Doug, and just be here for your kids. Let us do our job."

"I want to go with you, please," said Doug. *"I can help."*

"Doug, you know we can't let you do that. You're too emotionally tied to this."

With that Sgt. Parker and Officer Trent got in the back seat of a squad car and were ushered away.

Doug had gleaned that Quinton shot—perhaps even killed—his very own son. And if that were true, he certainly wouldn't have spared Cynthia's life. Doug stepped out of the station for some fresh air. His pragmatic, professional side was telling him Cynthia was dead, but he didn't want to believe that. His emotional side was telling him she could be fighting for her life and could make it through . . . like Taylor.

Doug leaned up against the façade of the small police station and began to sob. Everything that he had been holding back for the past five days completely exploded. Twenty-five years of police experience told him Cynthia was gone. He could no longer pretend things were okay in front of his children when his whole world was crashing down on him, no matter how hard he tried.

Doug returned to a very small conference room where Paul and Taylor were sitting. Both could tell their father had been crying.

"What is it, Dad? Do we know what's happened to Mom? Is she dead, Dad?"

"No, I haven't heard anything, but it's not looking good for us, kids," Doug spoke tenderly to them.

"We need to pray and pray hard for your mother. My guess is we will know something soon."

A female officer, Ann Caffory, introduced herself and asked if she could get them anything to drink. All three declined. She was very kind and offered to do anything she could to make them more comfortable.

An hour which seemed more like a day went by and Officer Caffory returned to the room and told them there was someone who came to visit them. In walked Jim Pascoe and his wife Holly.

"Jim, Holly, how did you get here? How did you know . . . ?"

"The how's don't matter, Doug. We're here and we're not leaving until you come back with us."

There was a long, enduring group hug. Taylor found relief in holding on to Holly. She had a motherly touch and tender smile. Paul needed uplifting too, but it made him feel good that the pastor was here for his dad who was in even greater need of encouragement and strength. His dad had stayed strong for so long—probably for him and Taylor— but now he seemed to be falling apart. Both Jim and Holly had a comforting, calming spirit. Jim asked if they could offer up a prayer for the family. He and Holly both took turns sharing the Conrad concerns with God, asking for peace and comfort and help during this time of fear and uncertainty. Shortly after they were done praying and the family sat around discussing the last several hours, there was a knock at the door and Agent Brewster and D'Andrea walked in with grim faces.

Without saying a word, tears started streaming down Doug's face and Taylor let out a scream that came from the deepest crevice of her soul. Paul sat frozen. Both men pulled up a seat and with the most sincere but gut wrenching tone, Agent Brewster announced that they had found Cynthia's body in the woods. She had been shot once in the back, probably running for her life. They would need Doug to go with them to identify her body.

Doug held on to Paul and Taylor as all three sobbed. Jim's arms were around Doug's shoulders and Holly had both of her arms embracing both children. Despite the deep sadness, they were also feeling the love and sympathy pour out to them by their dearest friends and the officers. They had prayed that this event would have a happy ending, but it was not meant to be. It ended tragically as most of these cases do. After they stood there and wept for quite some time, the agents apologized for not being able to have found her in time. They offered assurances that they would find the perpetrator who did this, and that an APB was out for Quinton Reed. They promised not to give up until he was found and arrested for Cynthia's murder.

Once the children were able to gain control of their emotions, Paul asked if he and Taylor could go with him to see their mother. Doug told them it would be the toughest experience of their lives, but if they felt they could do it, it was okay with him. Jim assured Doug he and Holly would be right there for them.

Doug realized that someone had made arrangements to notify and get the Pascoes here for his family, and for that he was truly grateful. He didn't know any of the logistics, but Doug realized that all divisions of the police force did everything they could for him and his family. They empathized with him, and now all that could be done was to comfort them. Doug had no time to think about Quinton Reed. He would have to deal with him later. Now he was focused on seeing Cynthia. He would have to brace himself for seeing this vibrant, beautiful woman lying on a concrete slab, being prepared for an autopsy. The thought was unbearable—several days ago they were enjoying dinner together, laughing, and later that night making love. Who could have known their week would have ended this way—so senselessly, so tragically?

He had been in the morgue numerous times, but never for a loved one. And never with his children. He knew that life would be different for his children forever after today. His heart ached as much for them as it ached for himself. Their faith would have to sustain them, and they were being put to the test.

CHAPTER 62

They were taken to the Parkersburg County Morgue and as soon as they arrived they were escorted to the floor by Agent Brewster.

Doug turned to his kids.

"You don't have to come in unless you want to. I assure you, it won't make you feel better. This will be the most difficult thing you will probably ever do in your lifetime."

"We want to see her, Dad. No matter what."

"Okay. Let's go in."

The assistant to the coroner already had the gurney pulled out with a sheet over the body. In the most kind and gentle way, he admonished them not to touch the body as they had not gleaned all of the necessary evidence. Once the family gathered around the gurney, he pulled the sheet back, exposing Cynthia's face and upper shoulders.

Both children let out a mournful gasp and quickly looked away. Doug's gaze was fixed on Cynthia's bruised cheek but still beautiful face. He took in every detail of her face. Agent Brewster took Taylor and Paul by the shoulders and led them out into the hallway to a waiting area. Holly and Jim were there to offer any help they could.

The coroner stepped to the back of the room and let Doug have his private moment. He witnessed Doug bending over Cynthia near her face and stepped closer to confirm he wasn't touching her. Doug was whispering to Cynthia with a gut wrenching, choking whisper.

" Even in death, you are so beautiful. Oh, Cynthia, I should have been there to protect you. I'm so sorry, sweetheart. I failed you . . . Oh, Cynthia . . . Cynthia . . . my love."

The assistant stepped forward and put his hand on Doug's arm.

"I'm so sorry for your loss, sir. Is this your wife, Cynthia Conrad?"

In an almost inaudible moan that the assistant had heard a myriad of other times, he heard Doug say, *"Yes, this is Cynthia Conrad, my wife."*

"We'll do everything we can to provide the scientific facts needed in this case in order to put the guilty party away, Mr. Conrad. You have our word on that."

"Thank you. I appreciate it."

Doug desperately wanted to linger longer with Cynthia, but he knew the identification had been completed and now his children needed him worse. When he stepped out of the room reluctantly, he saw his children with the Pascoes and Mitch Neubauer.

"Mitch."

He was really no more surprised to see Mitch there than he was the Pascoes. These were probably his dearest friends ever. It was clear that an entire team was working together to support him and his children, and to see that the needs of his family were being met. How all of this had happened and so quickly would be for another time, but right now he just knew he was glad they were all here for him and his children.

"Doug, I'm so sorry we couldn't save her in time. How are you doing, good buddy?"

" I'm overwhelmed, Mitch. It was her. Somehow I was still holding out that it wouldn't be her. She was shot in the back. What sick coward shoots a woman and shoots her in the back?" Tears were flowing down Doug's cheeks. As Mitch studied his face and the anguish on it, he thought his friend looked like he had aged ten years.

Mitch embraced Doug.

" As soon as I made some calls and confirmed what had happened here in West Virginia, I asked my brother-in-law to fly me and the Pascoes here. By then, I already knew the circumstances, Doug. I knew

you would need us. I'm so sorry, Doug. I am so so sorry. We will solve this case. We now know who we're looking for, so he won't get away with this. It's just a matter of time. Every cop around the country is looking for Quinton Reed."

CHAPTER 63

The death and circumstances were all over the national news. Quinton Reed's picture was plastered on television screens everywhere, and the murders of Cynthia Conrad and Brady Randolph had been relegated to headline news. Kevin Reed was in critical condition fighting for his life at Camden-Clark Memorial Hospital. A guard was assigned outside his hospital room. Calls were pouring in inquiring as to what his role was in this crime while the talk show hosts were interpolating what should happen to this accomplice. Public condolences were expressed to both the Conrad and Randolph families by the governors of both West Virginia and Ohio as well as the public. Enraged TV viewers opined freely about what should be done to the killers.

Meanwhile, Ramona Reed had refused any comment by the press as she left her home with her two other sons to travel to West Virginia to be at Kevin's bedside. She couldn't believe that she had gone from an unknown person to a heavily pursued woman by local and national TV reporters. She was still baffled as to how Kevin got tied up with Quinton or what Kevin's role was in this entire mess. She couldn't believe that her gentle son could have done the things that the press was saying he had done. However, all she could dwell on now was her son's own survival. She would focus on his criminal involvement later.

The news first broke when the police knocked at her door to tell her of Kevin's serious condition and location. The policeman was accompanied by a police detective with a psychology background who wanted to learn more about Quinton so that they could develop a better profile that would assist them in finding him.

Ramona was absolutely shocked that Quinton shot their son and addressed that surprise. Of all the things Quinton was, he had never been terribly mean to the kids. He directed most of his anger and deprecations toward her or women in general and anyone in authority over him. He was a narcissist. Life revolved around Quinton, and anyone who wronged him or crossed him in some way had to suffer or pay a penalty.

The detective formulated a profile of Quinton and returned to the station to conduct some important meetings and teleconferences with the West Virginia agents. While Quinton wasn't well educated, he wasn't stupid. He most likely had learned a wealth of information from his prison inmates the past fifteen years, so he would be street smart, for sure. Knowing Quinton's family background and his probable mental state, it was thought he might follow one of two paths. Clearly his goal would be to not get caught, and to leave the country the first chance he could get. But he did have a conscience about some things and a mindset about justice, so now the detectives were formulating some possible moves Quinton might make. Either Quinton would try to visit his son at the hospital, which was quite risky, or finish his job to kill the rest of the Conrad family and then leave the country. Quinton's crimes had escalated into a death penalty case, and he would know that. Therefore, he didn't have much to lose in the end. Rather than be incarcerated again and face the death penalty, he would, most likely, not willingly surrender alive if apprehension was at hand.

Quinton was a very dangerous person to the public at this point, so the joined teams devised two plans that might draw him out and began putting them in place.

CHAPTER 64

Doug Conrad with his children were driven to the Parkersburg Police Department to go through the procedures and logistics of the next several days regarding Cynthia's remains and when her body would be released to the family for burial. Paul and Taylor were then asked to step out of the room and join the Pascoes while they had a private moment with their dad.

Agents Brewster and D'Andrea along with Officers Preston and Trent and the West Virginia authorities now involved in the case wanted to have a brainstorming session with Doug to see how they could draw out Quinton Reed without more people getting hurt or killed.

Quinton Reed's profile had been faxed from Akron to them quickly and reviewed by Agent Marcia McCall, Parkersburg's most adroit psychological profiler. While Doug had been visiting the morgue, their team had discussed several plans that might bring the killer out into the open. If one of the plans was agreed upon by Doug Conrad, they could begin the necessary steps of engagement. Neither plan, however, would be without risk and cost.

CHAPTER 65

THE PROPOSAL

Agent Brewster began the meeting, introducing all of the parties around the conference table.

"Doug, Detective McCall who has a degree in psychology and is trained in criminal profiling, has reviewed a preliminary profile of Quinton Reed from agents in Akron. With that information, our team has come up with two or three possible plans that may bring Quinton Reed to us. If we can get cooperation from the press, we will immediately put our plans to work. So, I'm going to turn the rest of the meeting over to Detective McCall."

"Sir, we want you and your family to know how sorry we are about your wife. We know your entire family has been through so much in the past few days. We know your family has been threatened by the person we believe to be Quinton Reed, so we, like you, want him caught before anyone else gets hurt. Here are some things we know about Mr. Reed:

#1   He is pompous and self-centered
#2   He displays manipulative and exploitive behaviors in order to get his own way
#3   He has an insatiable need for control

#4   *He is unwilling to take blame for anything that goes wrong in his life or to acknowledge reality*

#5   *He displays angry outbursts in order to intimidate others and get his way*

#6   *He is selfish and driven to come out on top by imposing his will on others, and more than likely that is how he drew his son, Kevin, into this mess. We know he will browbeat someone with a distorted sense of duty or obligation*

#7   *He demands loyalty from others; thus, the reason he probably shot his own son*

#8   *He is a liar*

#9   *He's condescending*

#10 *He will sometimes say what another person wants to hear but then acts contrary to what he actually said*

#11 *He has unbroken resolve, carrying a deep desire to finish his plan and win!*

Now that last one brings me to what I think his next move might be. Since his goal was to destroy your entire immediate family, we believe he still may attempt to do that for the sake of revenge. Succeeding, after all, is everything to a guy like Quinton. Are you with me so far?"

"Yes." Doug was listening attentively but was already anticipating what she was about to say next.

"Now Quinton may do it in one of two ways. He may either try to come after you, Paul, and Taylor—where you live. He may return to your home since he knows where you live and knows the inside of your home pretty well. This is where the press comes in. As we update the story on the news, we can provide information to Quinton and set him up. 'The Conrad family has now returned to their home to mourn the death of Cynthia Conrad and prepare for the burial of their beloved wife and mother.' He will believe all three of you are home, vulnerable with your guard down, and easy pickin's for him."

"So you want me to jeopardize the lives of my kids in their own home? I don't want my children traumatized any more than they already are, nor do I want them to be afraid to stay at our house. Remember, this all started at our home to begin with," argued Doug.

"Well, actually, none of you will be home. We will have police officers there posing as you three. They will be decoys. We will have hidden officers posted around the neighborhood watching for him and take him down before he can get a shot off."

"I want him to be taken alive. I want to face him in court and hear his story, and I want him to know he will never see the light of day again."

"You may not get that anyway, Mr. Conrad. It is a strong possibility that he would take his own life before allowing himself to be incarcerated again or face the death penalty."

"And your second plan?" asked Doug.

"We believe he may be audacious enough to actually disguise himself as a mourner and walk into the funeral home and try to kill all three of you at once."

"I don't want the visitation hours or funeral to be a circus. Nor could we jeopardize the lives of any of our family or friends. How would you go about protecting us?"

"Yes, we certainly agree. We would set up a fake funeral with police decoys and wait for him to show up. He wouldn't realize he was set up until he got inside the funeral home. There would be no escape for him as all doors would be guarded and locked from the inside. Perhaps, also, we could do a simple graveside memorial and post officers all around the grounds. There is a greater chance, however, for us to lose him out in the open.

"Our final plan is to announce Kevin Reed's death, even though it looks like he may pull through. We'll fake his death and do a graveside only. There's a slight chance he would show up for that. But since he feels his son betrayed him by letting Taylor escape, our success with that plan is dubious."

Agent D'Andrea interjected. *"Right now, Mr. Conrad, Mr. Reed is on the run. He knows we are all looking for him. We don't believe he has any contacts to provide him with a fake passport, so we are pretty sure he can't flee the country unless he smuggles himself into Mexico somehow. As soon as Kevin Reed is conscious and physically able, we will interrogate him and may be able to obtain some valid or clearly defined plan the two of them may have had."*

As Doug tried to scrutinize all of the plans and their possible consequences, he knew that the team was probably correct in their approach in order to put an expedient end to this case. He also knew which plan he preferred.

CHAPTER 66

Elaine Neubauer showed Taylor and Paul to their bedrooms and showed them where the guest bathroom was. She did everything possible to make them comfortable and yet respect their privacy.

She had lost her mother to a car accident when she was fourteen years old, so she had some idea as to what they were feeling. Murder seemed much worse, however, even though the end result was still the same. Sudden deaths are still a shock and are final. Like her mother, Cynthia wasn't going to come back.

By now each of them had probably tried to relive their mom's final moments and look at all of the things in their lives that mom would not be there for—college graduations, marriages, grandchildren, holidays. It would be an overwhelming adjustment, and, if that weren't enough, they were still targets with their very lives still in jeopardy.

Mitch's role was to protect Taylor and Paul so that Doug could concentrate on what he needed to do. Since their own children were grown and living on their own and Elaine had her CCW license, there was no problem hiding them away for several days until Quinton Reed could be found and arrested. Besides, Elaine had always loved the Conrad children so this plan seemed like the perfect plan. Mitch was sure it wouldn't take more than a day or two. After all, Quinton Reed was no cranial power, and he was bound to make a mistake even before a confrontation at the Conrad home.

Doug insisted on remaining at his own house with the decoy team *when* or *if* Quinton Reed showed up. Mitch went along with the plan except for that part. If something went wrong and Doug was killed, these kids would lose both parents. Doug was obstinate about it so the team reluctantly approved. It was impossible to tell the homeowner he couldn't stay in his own home. Doug was confident his presence in the house would bring Quinton to them—with the help of the media, that is.

The plan was carefully planned, weighed, and initiated.

CHAPTER 67

"*T*he Conrad family has returned home from Parkersburg, West Virginia after having made a positive ID of their wife and mother. They were hoping for a happy outcome as all of us were, so our hearts certainly reach out to them.

"We just spoke to the Conrad family in their home. Doug Conrad expressed his appreciation for everything the authorities and the press have done to bring this kidnapping to a close and now ask for privacy as he and his children mourn their loss and make funeral plans for Cynthia Conrad.

"Meanwhile Kevin Reed remains in a deep coma with very little chance for recovery. As you remember, he was shot by his own father, Quinton Reed, whom authorities are pursuing. The police have been unable to talk to Kevin or to learn the motive for the kidnappings of Cindy and Taylor Conrad and Cynthia's ultimate murder. They may never have the chance, but authorities believe Quinton Reed will try to flee the country.

"Kevin's father is the prime suspect in this crime. Here is what we believe he may look like, so if anyone sees Mr. Reed, he or she is asked to call 330-375-1000. He is armed and dangerous and should not be approached. This is Erin Wright at Channel 3 News."

CHAPTER 68

Quinton stood in the dark shadows of the bar listening to the news on their mounted TV. Before anyone recognized him, he would need to get to his car. Going any place, now, and being unrecognized would be impossible. He would need to resort to a disguise.

The six men and one woman sitting at the bar seemed pretty buzzed, so he felt confident no one had thought much about the newscast nor imagined they were only ten feet away from the Wanted Man on the TV screen. Fortunately, he had kept a low profile and his face turned away from the other patrons. He polished off his second Budweiser and left Bugsy's Roadhouse Tavern.

Breaking in a drugstore or a Dollar General was risky, but he didn't have much of a choice. He would need several ball caps, a windbreaker or any change of clothing, hair dyes, whatever he could find to help him move around town incognito. He would steal enough food so he didn't need to stop at a fast food and risk being recognized.

He couldn't believe he had allowed himself to get in this dilemma, and he had his son to thank for all of this. If he just hadn't let the girl go, none of this would have happened. It would have been nice to see his son and spend a few hours with him, but he really didn't mean to drag the boy into this crime. He hadn't actually meant to shoot his son, but his temper got away from him. He shot on impulse. Hopefully, Kevin can pull through and get out from under this with a fairly light sentence. He needed to put these thoughts aside now, and focus on his next step.

It was apparent to him from the news that he had made quite a name for himself since being released from prison, but his mission wasn't yet completed. Quite the contrary. He needed a safe place to hide while back in Akron so he could do just that. Ramona, Kalen and Kerry were probably at Kevin's bedside in West Virginia, so he knew which house would most likely be vacant for a few days. That would be sufficient time.

He would devise the perfect plan on his drive into the Akron area. Doug Conrad may think his ordeal is over but it was just beginning. He was going to be Doug Conrad's worst nightmare.

CHAPTER 69

"*D*amn! *This idiot is going to get us both put in prison!*"

Allen Stanwick had just listened to the local and national news and the Conrad story was the top story on both stations. If Quinton Reed had only stuck to Allen's plan, he would have earned a large amount of money and would be able to ride off into the sunset a free and rich man. But, no, he had to risk everything to satisfy his personal vendetta against Doug Conrad.

Quinton had lied to him about kidnapping Taylor Conrad, and he had believed him. Allen knew if Quinton got caught and arrested, he would try to make a deal with the authorities and incriminate Allen, even though he wasn't sure what Allen's crime was that he had hired him to obscure; he just knew it must have been *criminal*. Quinton also knew where Allen's weapon was, and if he produced the weapon that could surely prove closure for the McGrary/Stover murders.

Everything Allen had worked so hard for in his career could soon be coming to an end. While it was true he hired Quinton to abduct Cynthia Conrad in order to distract and delay Douglas Conrad from investigating the McGrary murder, he never expected nor ordered Cynthia to be hurt nor killed. Quinton veered from the plan altogether. Just being disbarred would be the least of Allen's worries. He would be convicted of accessory to Cynthia's murder if caught and would be incarcerated like street trash.

Allen's plan to use Ramona's ex-con ex-husband seemed like the logical choice at the time, but Allen had miscalculated the *criminal mind*. He might also be considered an accomplice in the hunter's murder and the abduction of Taylor Conrad—all felonies. He had no idea Quinton planned to commit any of these crimes. Quinton had no intentions of ever releasing Cynthia Conrad safely as planned. Police would never believe Allen once they found proof that he personally killed two innocent women for money. He was clearly facing the death penalty. Quinton double crossed him. However, if Quinton was unable to talk to the police and incriminate him, his problem would be resolved.

Greed had led Allen down a road that seemingly had no return. He would lose respect from his wife, his children, and the community if the truth was discovered. He couldn't turn to his Uncle Steve to get him out of this mess—not this time, nor could he turn to his father-in-law or the law firm to represent him. He had failed so many people. Well, his dad always told him, *"Never cry over spilled milk, son. Just clean it up and the quicker, the better."* Translated, Allen knew what must be done.

CHAPTER 70

Allen decided to call Ramona's house under the guise of seeing how Kevin was getting along, but what he was seeking was some inside information as to where the authorities were looking for Quinton or to see if she knew where he might be. Perhaps he even called her to see how Kevin was, even though that would have been risky.

The phone rang four times and then someone picked up, but without saying hello.

"*Ramona*?"

Dead silence.

"*Ramona*?" Still no answer.

Quinton recognized Allen's voice and smiled. Quinton knew the position he put Allen Stanwick in but felt absolutely no sympathy for him. In fact, his relationship with the Akron mayor's nephew gave him some leverage IF he got caught.

Allen hung up without saying anything more, but as he pondered who had picked up the phone at the other end but failed to speak, it occurred to him that it may have been Quinton. Was it possible? He wouldn't have any place to hide, and it appeared from the newscast that Ramona was in West Virginia staying by her critically wounded son. Quinton might be audacious enough to re-visit his home, but he would be taking a huge risk of getting caught by the authorities. After all, wouldn't that be a likely place for Quinton to turn to?

Allen checked his second favorite revolver, got in the car, and drove across town to Ramona's home. He parked a block away to study the house for awhile. No lights were on, but he spotted a Ford Taurus pulling out of the driveway. It was dark but Allen sensed that the driver might be Quinton. He decided to follow him from afar, and if given an opportunity, he would kill him.

The Taurus got off at the Massillon Rd. exit in Green, Ohio from I-77. It registered to Allen that the driver was indeed Quinton and he must be heading for the Conrad home. Surely, he wouldn't be that crazy or bold to think he could pull that off without getting caught. Police would probably be surrounding the house to further protect the Conrad family. Did Quinton think he could shoot his way into that house and live out his vendetta against Doug Conrad and his family? Doug was an experienced police officer and homicide investigator. He was intelligent and on high alert for protecting his family, especially now. Quinton was clearly an egomaniac and his level of stupidity was unequaled. He had to be stopped before he neared the Conrad home.

The Taurus drove two blocks passed the Conrad home and made a right turn around the corner onto another side street. Allen drove passed his car, turned left at the next road and turned around in a driveway. He turned off his headlights and parking lights and moved closer to the intersection so he could keep an eye on the Taurus. He pulled to the curb and turned the motor off. Allen knew he was out of his realm when dealing with an ex-con, so he had to be very careful. He was playing cat and mouse with a loaded gun, and he was quite sure Quinton was fully equipped as well.

The night was overcast and the moon was hardly visible. Fifteen minutes into the wait, Allen saw whom he believed to be Quinton get out of his car. He began to jog toward the Conrad residence at a leisurely pace. He was wearing a black sweatshirt, black shorts, Nike tennis shoes, and a black sweat head band around blond hair. Allen was beginning to have doubts that that was indeed Quinton. Could it be one of Ramona's other sons? But if it was, why had he driven to Green near the Conrad home just to jog? Something just wasn't adding up. He called Quinton's cell phone number, but it was out of service. He decided to get out of his car and follow this person, keeping a safe distance from him so as not to arouse curiosity or attention.

CHAPTER 71

Quinton somehow sensed that he was walking into a setup. He observed an unmarked car one block from the Conrad home. A young man not in uniform, who clearly looked like a rookie, sat behind the wheel of the car with his window down. It was a humid evening and he was talking on a police radio. Quinton moved slowly but literally crawled behind the vehicle.

"I've seen no activity so far. What makes the head honchos so sure this guy's going to show up tonight and try something?"

"The profilers seem to think his will is so strong to kill the rest of the Conrad family that he has to move in quickly and take his best shot. The media has a way of telling everything they know and putting folks in harm's way, but this time, they're working for us. Reed's being set up big time."

"What do you mean?" asked the rookie.

"Well, people have been led to believe that the Conrads are all home and planning the burial of Cynthia Conrad."

"Makes good sense since she's dead, after all. Where are the kids? I never did hear where they were hiding them?"

"Mitch Neubauer, Conrad's partner, is keeping the kids at his house for tonight. He lives in Manchester over there on Comet Road. Mitch was a great cop when he worked for us and then he decided investigative work was more interesting, so he and Doug Conrad started their own

business and have been quite successful. Mitch and his wife will take good care of those kids. I guess a squad car will also be circling the neighborhood throughout the night as an extra precaution for Mitch's home and alert him if any suspicious activity is seen. My brother-in-law lives right next door to them there on the corner of Caston and Provens. I told him to keep his eyes open for any unusual activity too. You can bet Mitch will be armed to the teeth and won't let anything happen to those kids. They suspect all the activity will occur at the Conrad home since none of this has been aired or discussed publicly."

"Well, thanks for the info. So far there's been no sighting of the perp, but I'll keep my eyes peeled for the s.o.b. Hope he does show up tonight. I'd like nothing better than to put a bullet through him and put the Conrads at ease forever."

Quinton realized his plans needed to be altered, but they would be very workable since he knew what he was dealing with. This young rookie was his new best friend. Quinton was able to crawl back behind the bushes without being seen, but he was prepared to kill the young man instantly if he spotted him. He returned to his car, but he thought he saw movement from his right peripheral vision. He paused to look in the direction but saw nothing suspicious. He had no time to investigate even though this was a time for caution and clear thinking. He didn't want to take anything for chance but he didn't want to look for trouble either.

Allen sensed Quinton was aware of the bushes in front of him moving and feared he would get caught. He needed to affront Quinton when he was least expecting it. Allen was naïve when it came to committing the *perfect crime* or coming up against someone like Quinton Reed. He needed to sneak up behind him and never allow any kind of physical altercation. He would need to shoot Quinton with a silencer and the first bullet needed to be lethal. Close range would be required.

CHAPTER 72

Quinton returned to his Taurus and dialed up 411 on his cell.

"Yes, operator, I need the home address of Mitch Neubauer who lives in Manchester on Caston Road."

"Yes, sir. That number is 448 Caston Road. Is there anything else I can help you with sir?"

"No, thanks. You were a big help."

He slowly pulled away from the curb and found a remote parking lot where he could study a map. Good. It couldn't be more than fifteen minutes away from where he was now. Quinton smiled, anxious to see all of their surprised faces when he stepped inside the house with The Judge.

CHAPTER 73

Four armed police officers were hidden and out of view in the Conrad home. Some of the curtains and drapes were drawn to make it look like the normal night setting while some of the blinds were left up and some of the curtains open so that anyone outside could see in.

One female officer about the size of Taylor with dark hair was poised to be Taylor. She was positioned in the living room on the couch, wearing jeans and looking very collegiate but armed with a knife, handcuffs, and a loaded Glock 22. A young male officer who mimicked Paul in appearance was sitting at the kitchen table, eating snacks and enjoying a Coke. Both officers wore bullet proof vests under their clothes and were on high alert as they knew they were the targets. They had plenty of back up. In fact, it would take a lot for the perpetrator to get past the hidden security force staggered throughout the neighborhood without being seen. Nevertheless, Quinton Reed was high on the list of The Most Wanted right now and was a person to be reckoned with.

Doug Conrad walked around the house as he normally would, but he worried about his kids. He knew they were safe at Mitch's, but he would be relieved when Reed was finally captured and would no longer be a threat to them. He hoped and prayed Reed would attempt to break in the Conrad home tonight, so this heinous ordeal could be put in the past. He needed to bury his wife and get his home back to some level of normalcy, whatever that was. Nothing had been normal for the last five days.

He, too, was wearing a bullet proof vest and had a concealed weapon on him. This was all so surreal. He really didn't want a confrontation with Quinton. If he had the opportunity to kill him, he wouldn't hesitate, but the rage he felt inside wasn't a feeling he felt comfortable with. He knew it would take months if not years to remove the bitterness and hatred toward Quinton. Living with anger and hatred was never a good thing, but his loss was so great. His children's loss was so great. It could never be regained. Quinton Reed took all of that away from him.

Doug strolled from room to room in his house. So many memories came to mind in each room. The interior decorating itself was a reflection of Cynthia's love for her family, and she did it so well—from photographs and pictures on the wall to the color schemes and accessories. Everything was so comfortable and exquisite.

Now and then Doug would walk past an open window and tarry, hoping in some ways to tempt Quinton and draw him out of his dark hole, and yet, he needed to protect himself. His kids needed him. The last thing he wanted was for them to be traumatized further and experience another deep loss.

He needed to keep focused on the goal for tonight. A lot of officers who had been his friends for years had volunteered to give up their free time and help set the prey for Quinton Reed. He felt their love and support and even sympathy, but despite all of that, he was troubled. As the evening wore on, something troubled Doug. He couldn't pinpoint what it was, but something just didn't feel right. It was getting late, and Quinton Reed had not made an appearance.

CHAPTER 74

The Neubauer home was a four bedroom colonial home set on a three quarter acre lot. The houses in their allotment were evenly spaced and it was a Home Watch Neighborhood. Mitch had organized it himself, and it had proven a good thing. Over the years there had been only one burglary since the signs had come up and the neighbors were committed to watching the comings and goings more closely.

Not even the neighbors on each side of Mitch were aware he was harboring the Conrad children tonight. It was a clandestine operation. Neubauer knew his immediate neighbors on either side of his home were quite vigilant, and he hoped if there was an event tonight, he would be forewarned by one of their observations. However, the situation was quite serious, and he didn't want to lure them into jeopardy in any way, so it was better they not know. In any event, he was pretty sure the kids would be quite safe, but he worried that the Conrad home wouldn't be equally as quiet.

Paul and Taylor went to their respective rooms just down the hall from the master bedroom. Their bedroom lights were out as Mitch passed by. It was 11 p.m. and Elaine was taking her shower and preparing for bed.

Mitch was restless. Very restless—burdened with the responsibility of keeping the Conrad children safe. He knew Doug was carrying the heaviest load, and he was more than willing to help his best friend and partner. To be responsible for the safety of his two children while knowing an ex-con was plotting to kill both and would stop at nothing, was the highest compliment Doug could have paid him. It also motivated him to stay on high alert.

Mitch was confident in his professional skills. He had been trained militarily before heading to the Persian Gulf as well as the police academy and Quantico. He had earned a black belt in karate and had always been active in the Zeppelin Rifle Club. He competed in shooting tournaments whenever he had time and won quite a few trophies. Having been a private investigator for the past ten years had given him the nose of a blood hound. He could sniff out trouble, sense danger, and let his curiosity lead him to the right places. He always felt he had a *sixth sense* that had kept him alive during a few close calls in his career. Tonight he walked around his house on *high alert* and wasn't about to let anything happen to Taylor nor Paul. They had been through a lot in the past five days, and he wanted them to be able to put this horrible tragedy behind them. He had known these kids since they were babies and knew they would carry this tragedy with them for life. How could they not? But the fear of their family peril continuing compounded, adding to their anxieties and it had to end. Mitch hoped tonight would be the night.

Their home security system had been activated for the door sensors only as Mitch would be patrolling the house throughout the night. The lights had been turned off downstairs with the exception of carefully positioned night lights in each room. Mitch decided to make one last tour of the downstairs checking the locks on every door and window and observing the yard around the entire house. He had motion detector lights positioned outside their glass slider leading from the patio to the kitchen to alert him to any nearby movement, so he felt no one could sneak up on them without him being aware of their proximity. He closed the vertical blind.

Mitch never intended to get much sleep tonight. He planned to rest in his big Lazy Boy recliner in the great room and make rounds every hour on the hour. He was armed, had his cell phone on and in his pocket, and all land phones were charged and working. He knew Elaine would be sleeping lightly tonight also and that her gun was on a shelf at the headboard just above her pillow.

Mitch looked out a window at the front of his house. The street looked deserted. None of the neighbors had company in their driveways and only a few lights were on in one house down the street. He walked to the dining room window and looked out. A row of arborvitaes trees separated their yard from the Joyner's. He could see between two of them and saw a light just going off in the Joyner's kitchen. Bob and Rachel had probably just finished watching the 10 o'clock news, were taking their night pills, and heading upstairs for bed.

Mitch quietly moved to the great room and looked out that window one more time before returning to his Lazy Boy chair and settling in for the night. Few stars were out tonight, but the leaves on the big oak were blowing, confirming the weatherman's report that a thunderstorm was on the way. Shadows of the leaves were dancing on the ground, but Mitch felt comfortable nothing was amiss.

He had put on some loose fitting sweat pants and a tee shirt to wear for the night. He put on a clean pair of sweat socks and his Nike Air Max Edge shoes sat on the floor beside the recliner should he need to slip into them quickly. He settled in to the comfy chair and brought up the stool, pushing back in the chair. His Smith and Wesson .38 special was loaded and sitting openly on the end table beside his chair. The house was quiet except for the ticking of the large grandfather clock on the wall.

Mitch tried to relax but was just too uptight about the events of the past tragic days. He could only imagine what Doug was going through right now. He had been right alongside Doug since this whole ordeal began, but unless it is your wife who was kidnapped, raped, and shot in the back, or your daughter drugged and abducted where her fate could have been the same, you can't fully appreciate the depth of the emotions. One day your life is in order, the career and business is thriving, things are going well for the family, the marriage is terrific, and then . . . the one person who means everything to you has been snuffed out by riffraff.

Life wasn't fair.

CHAPTER 75

A police car drove slowly by the Neubauer home and didn't see anything suspicious. The officer would drive by in another hour or so.

Quinton watched him pass by from the shadows of two evergreen trees. He knew he needed to move quickly. He wound his way around the house opposite the side with the motion detector light. He saw the ADT signs posted on the windows and the sign near the front door, and rightly assumed the security system was engaged. He figured the cop was armed to the teeth. Conrad's kids wouldn't be, but they may have been given a big club or hammer to use for protection. No match for The Judge. He also carried Randolph's filet knife so he could quietly kill his two victims and leave. He liked options.

Prison time had been an opportunity to talk to lots of felons and learn of their mistakes during crimes that had landed them there. Mistakes they would never make again. These were far more serious felons than Quinton had ever been. But the lessons were there, and he learned them very well.

One lesson he had learned was the different ways of by-passing a security system. He also learned that the average home owner with one only has the main floor secured, so that when upstairs , family members can move around to the various rooms without setting it off. Just for lack of time and knowing that cops aren't rich, he was going to assume that was this household's set up. However, if he miscalculated, he knew he could make a quick escape. But for right now, he would mete out his revenge and then leave the country. That had always been his plan. The same way the Mexicans were sneaking across the borders into the U.S. would be the same path he would take to sneak into their country. He had the plan carefully mapped out.

Quinton had studied the back of the Neubauer home for hours and had watched the upstairs lights going on and off until he was pretty sure he knew which windows went to bedrooms and a bathroom. It had been raining and thundering for the last half hour, which was good. It might drown out any noise he might make while entering the home. The storm could, however, keep light sleepers awake, so he needed to be alert. Due to the circumstances, they would probably be too nervous to sleep soundly.

Once the household lights were off for quite some time, allowing everyone to fall soundly asleep, Quinton was ready to enter the upstairs bathroom window. A large tree near the house had been his original plan for helping him reach the upstairs as it was an easy tree to climb; however, neighbors two doors down had a twelve foot long ladder leaning on the side of their garage which would accommodate Quinton perfectly. He carried the ladder over to the bathroom window. The ladder legs sunk into the saturated ground but once he stabilized it, he began to ascend. He had a glass cutter on him and a suction cup.

He would know in seconds whether he needed to quickly retreat or could continue.

He took his glass cutter and cut out a small area around the window lock. The suction cup pulled the chunk of glass out quietly. Quinton reached inside to release the window lock. He heard a click, and very gently raised the window. Nothing went off. Good. He stepped inside. It was like Motel 6 where they even left the light on for him. The night light on the wall by the sink illuminated the room sufficiently so he didn't even need to use his *super duper clunk—over—the head* flashlight. The bathroom was quite large. It had a bathtub/shower with a thick, decorative shower curtain. He peaked behind it to make sure no one was lurking there or that he was being set up. No one. This was going to be fairly easy and a quick kill, or should he say *kills*. Nevertheless, he was going to have to be alert and very careful.

Lightning was flashing, thunder was clapping, and the rain pounded on the roof and spouting. Quinton couldn't have asked for better working conditions as he made his way out of the bathroom. Just as he took his final step from the bathroom to the hallway, the linoleum floor beneath him creaked really loudly. He stopped immediately and listened. All was still. He took his flashlight and aimed it down the hallway to both the left and right. Moving to the right of the hallway would lead to one bedroom and the staircase leading downstairs. Moving to the left would lead to three more doors. He moved to the right and just flashed down the staircase in case it would be easier to escape from there should things go wrong. No time to climb ladders. He took two or three steps down the stairs just to see if he could figure out the layout but not far enough to set off any alarm.

Mitch was sitting in his recliner, re-thinking the events of the past six days when he saw a flash of light move along the stairwell. What he saw was clearly not lightning. Every bedroom upstairs had a flashlight for safety reasons, but no one in the house would have been using them to come down the stairs. They would just put the hall light on and come down. This was very odd.

The hairs on the back of Mitch's neck stood up, and he began to get an adrenaline rush. His *sixth sense* was stirring within him. Was he over-reacting? He didn't think so. If someone had entered the house without setting off the alarm, then he had to have entered from upstairs. Mitch now regretted not having upstair window sensors installed. If Mitch called for back-up, the assailant would hear him talking, so there was no time for that.

He quietly got out of his chair and went to the side of the staircase so anyone looking down couldn't see him. His gun was drawn. He listened for movement. The thunder and rain was making it hard if, indeed, there was someone upstairs. Not only were the Conrad kids upstairs who were under his protective care, but his own wife was up in their room. He had jeopardized his own wife's life. He certainly didn't want to share the same loss as Doug. He and Elaine had been married for twenty-nine years, and he had every intention of taking her to Hawaii for their 30th wedding anniversary. Surely his eyes and ears were fooling him, but his professional training and knowledge of such situations were too serious to ignore.

As he quietly mounted the stairs, he noticed wet footprints on the beige carpet of the top two steps. His suspicions now were pretty much confirmed. Someone from outside this house was now inside and his name was most likely Quinton Reed.

CHAPTER 76

Mitch couldn't imagine how Quinton knew the Conrad kids were at his house. It was such a clandestine plan, and everyone on this case was sure Quinton would try attacking the Conrad home in hopes of getting all three of them at once.

When Mitch agreed to the plan, he never believed for a minute he was putting his own wife in jeopardy. He never feared for himself, and he knew that back up was not far away. But as he learned over the years through his job, the only thing *expected* with criminals is the *unexpected.*

It couldn't have been easy for Quinton to have entered their house from the upstairs and especially without waking up someone. He had to have come in via the guest bathroom window without gaining the attention of either Taylor, Paul, or Elaine.

Mitch figured Quinton had quickly learned the upstairs layout and was ready to enter a room. If he remained silent, none of them would be alerted to their imminent danger. He needed to call out a warning so a 911 call could be made or an escape effort could be initiated by all of them. Elaine could hit the panic button on the security pad in the bedroom provided she had the time and opportunity to reach it. The outdoor siren and strobe would go on, thus signaling the officer patrolling his home and the neighbors that they were in trouble.

Quinton would probably assume Mitch was also in the bedroom and try to avoid going in. If he could enter the kids' rooms and kill them undetected, his mission would be fulfilled and he would leave as quietly as he entered. Why take the chance, right?

But what if Quinton had already been able to discern he was downstairs? Then the other inhabitants upstairs would be more vulnerable.

Mitch knew that what he was about to do would most likely alert Quinton to his proximity and the awareness of his presence, but he hit the button on his cell phone anyway that called Doug Conrad's cell. If he didn't talk, Doug would know instantly it was him and there was a reason for his silence. The back up cops would be alerted and help would arrive, but whether soon enough was dubious.

When trouble breaks open, a shoot out can be over in seconds even if it feels like time stands still. Seconds can be never ending.

Mitch whispered a prayer and then hit the already programmed number for Doug's phone. Mitch returned the cell phone to his side pocket so that Doug could hear everything going on and respond accordingly. Mitch was about to turn the hall light switch on at the top of the steps with his gun aimed and ready should someone be there. The step he was mounting squeaked and Quinton turned back to the staircase, surprised that someone was coming up from downstairs. Not something he had calculated. He quietly moved to the top of the staircase and sensed that someone was no more than two feet away.

"Quinton is upstairs!" he yelled. Just then Quinton came out of the shadow and fired The Judge at Mitch before he could press his trigger. The impact of the bullet felt like a missile penetrating him. Mitch's gun crashed to the floor and just before he fell unconscious, he realized he was falling backward down the stairs.

It was too dark for Quinton to see where he hit the cop, but he knew he would no longer be a problem. The blast from his gun would have been a warning to the entire household, so he knew he had to act quickly. He would need to round them all up before anyone could make a phone call and kill them, leaving no witnesses. He figured the kids would panic and cower, so his biggest threat would probably be the cop's wife. The master bedroom would certainly have a phone. He needed to incapacitate her first and then find the son, his second biggest threat.

Elaine heard the gun go off and was absolutely stunned. For a split second she froze with fear. She then screamed for Mitch and immediately grabbed her gun and rushed toward the security pad by the door leading to the hallway. Before she could press the emergency button, the bedroom door flew open. Elaine wasn't sure if it was Mitch, the kids, or Quinton and, thus, hesitated pointing her gun. In her conceal carry class, she learned that a person might only have a second to react but that you never shoot without seeing your target. Who she shot mattered to her. Unfortunately, in Quinton's mind, everyone in the house became his enemy and a threat. Shoot on sight.

Elaine tried to get out a scream but before she could, Quinton came down on her head with his Judge like a sledgehammer. She slumped to the floor and into darkness.

Taylor was in the next bedroom listening to the loud commotion and realized she and Paul were in imminent danger.

She screamed for Paul and rushed toward the bedroom window, preparing to jump from the second floor if need be. If only she and Paul had shared the same room for one night only, they would have been together and able to protect each other. If she jumped out the window, what assurances did she have that someone perhaps working with Quinton wasn't down below waiting for her? What if, when she fell to the ground, she broke a leg and wouldn't be able to run and escape? It could be worse IF she jumped. If she stayed, Paul could help her perhaps or vice versa.

She put the window up and looked down, glancing around quickly. Then she chose to return to the bedroom door and listen.

She heard the man walk past her bedroom to Paul's bedroom door. Both of their bedroom doors were locked from the inside. She heard him try turning the door knob and then heard a gun blast and could tell he was blasting the door open. If he got in and Paul hadn't made it to the window in time to jump, he would surely be killed.

Paul was her brother, her only sibling. He had always been her buffer and protector, and now he needed help. She could never escape and save her own life and let him get killed without trying to help.

Without a further thought, she threw the door open and saw Quinton stepping into Paul's bedroom with his gun pointing into the room. She wasn't sure exactly where Paul was inside the room, but if he hadn't managed to jump out the window by now, he was surely trapped and his fate was certain.

"*Paul*!" she screamed.

Just then Quinton turned toward her with the gun pointing at her. Paul came from behind the door swinging a bat with such fury. It made instant contact with Quinton's head and right shoulder. Blood splattered across Taylor's face and neck. The look of surprise swept across Quinton's face for a split second and he dropped to the floor.

"*Oh my God! Oh, my God!*" screamed Taylor as she took a step backward at the sight of the horror.

Paul took the bat and came down on Quinton's right arm. They both heard a bone crack.

"*Here's another one for my Mom!*" Paul yelled out. The bat came down on his left arm. Again, both of them heard another bone crack. Quinton wasn't moving.

Taylor was beyond fear now and sobbing.

"*Paul, stop, stop!*" She bent down and picked up Quinton's gun. It was heavier than she had expected but at least it was out of the man's reach.

Paul continued to gaze at Quinton lying on the floor, blood gushing from his head. Clearly both arms were bent in unnatural positions, and a large bone was actually protruding from his upper right arm.

Taylor could see that if Quinton opened his eyes or even attempted to move a muscle, Paul was going to bash him with the bat once again. A look of total terror was on Paul's face. Neither was sure if Quinton was dead or not.

Taylor stepped over Quinton's body and put her arms around Paul.

"I think it's finally over, Paul. Enough people have died. You saved us. You surely saved us! Drop the bat, Paul. It's okay. He can't hurt us anymore!"

Paul refused to drop the bat.

"We need to check on Mr. and Mrs. Neubauer, Paul. I think they may be dead."

Sirens could be heard close by. Paul and Taylor realized the police were coming so someone in the house had been able to get a call off for help. Unfortunately, it hadn't come soon enough.

Paul was completely numb, unsure if he had killed Quinton. This man had killed his mother and deserved to die just as his mom had, but he wanted the man to actually live so he could be tried in a court of law and explain why he killed her. He wanted to confront him. Paul didn't regret beating Quinton with the bat. It was certainly and undeniably self-defense, but he knew his life was changed forever if he killed Quinton. He was still in shock at the events of tonight and was unsure just how really bad things were. He was almost afraid to know if both Mr. and Mrs. Neubauer were dead.

Taylor was shaking uncontrollably. One arm was around Paul and Quinton's gun was still in her other hand.

The front door downstairs burst open.

"Police! Come out with your hands up!"

Two police officers saw Mitch Neubauer at the base of the steps. He was bleeding profusely and was unconscious, but he was breathing.

"Officer down! We need medical help here ASAP!"

The other officer searched the entire main floor before motioning upstairs.

Paul yelled out.

"My sister and I are upstairs. I don't know if Mrs. Neubauer is dead or alive, but I think I might have killed Quinton Reed."

"Coming up. Stay where you are. Set down any weapons and keep your hands visible and up in the air," the officer commanded.

Taylor laid the gun down on the floor in the hallway, four feet away from Quinton while Paul set the bat down on the floor.

Just then Doug Conrad came storming into the Neubauer house with some of the officers who had been with him at the Conrad home.

"Paul! Taylor! It's Dad! Are you all right?" he cried out uncontrollably.

As soon as Doug saw Mitch, he rushed to him, calling out his name.

"Mitch! Mitch! Oh, buddy, I'm so sorry. Help is coming. Hang in there."

Doug was on his knees checking Mitch for signs of life and detected a slight pulse and feint breathing. Mitch had lost a lot of blood and needed to get to the hospital immediately. Just as Doug started to get up, the paramedics arrived and aimed straight for Mitch. Doug was halfway up the stairs as he heard another officer shout.

"We need more paramedics up here! We have two more people seriously injured . . . maybe dead!"

"Identify yourselves." he heard the officer inquire.

"We're Taylor and Paul Conrad," Taylor answered with apprehension.

Just then Doug Conrad and two other officers arrived at the top of the steps. Doug rushed to his children.

"These are my kids, officer! These are my kids!" Doug glanced around and saw Quinton's body on the floor, and as he looked just ahead, he saw Elaine's body slumped on the floor in a pool of blood at the doorway of her bedroom.

Doug put his arms around Paul and Taylor. Both were crying as was Doug.

Doug watched as one officer was leaning over Elaine. Doug broke from the grasp of his children and went over to Elaine. He bent down next to the police officer. He gently took Elaine's hand and whispered, *"Hang in there, Elaine. We're going to all make it through this. I'm so sorry for involving you and Mitch. We didn't know. We didn't know! I will make it up to you. I promise."*

"She's alive but she has a serious head wound. We need a paramedic up here pronto!" shouted one of the officers who had come up the stairs with Doug.

Just then paramedics were at the top of the steps with a gurney and another set of paramedics with a second gurney. The entire upstairs looked like a war zone.

Doug returned to his children who were now sitting on Taylor's bed in her bedroom.

"Are you both all right? Are either of you physically hurt?" Doug asked.

Both were too drained to even speak but both nodded that they weren't. Doug and another officer directed Taylor and Doug to come downstairs and sit in a squad car. They would need to go to the E.R. to be examined and then fill out a police report there. It was going to be a very long night, but it was the beginning of a new life . . . a safe life from now on. But it would be a changed life for everyone involved, including the Neubauers.

"Dad, did I kill the guy who killed Mom? I wanted to, Dad. He tried to kill Taylor. He would have killed us all. Are the Neubauers dead?" Paul was still in shock. It was obvious. He needed some time to settle down.

How would Doug ever forgive himself for putting his kids through this? He could never put the pieces of their lives back together again. In all of his years as a police officer and detective, he had never killed anyone in the line of duty. Not sure what the medical status was on Quinton, his young son may have killed him. Quinton not only killed Paul's mother but robbed his son of his innocence. Paul was going to need counseling. This he knew for sure. Taylor would probably need it as well, but certainly Paul would.

"They're alive, Paul, but they look like they're hurt pretty badly. The paramedics are working on them inside the ambulances. Once they stabilize them, they'll rush them to the hospital. I'm not sure about Quinton, son. His death won't be a loss to any of us, but we'll go to the hospital and wait with Mitch and Elaine's family until we hear the doctors' assessments of their condition, okay? We need to pray for them. As for Quinton, even if he does die, the authorities wouldn't press charges against you as it was self-defense. We'll deal with him later, son.

"I need to call Jim Pascoe. Are you both sure you're not hurt?" Doug asked once again.

"We're fine, Dad. Really." answered Taylor.

"Well, we need to get you both checked in ER, nonetheless."

"Mr. Conrad, we have a squad car waiting to take the three of you to Summa Hospital. Officers Preston and Parker will meet you there. You have two brave kids, sir. I'm glad it turned out for your good tonight, but I'm sorry for the loss of your wife," said the officer whose name Doug didn't know.

As the three Conrads stepped out of the Neubauer home to enter the squad car, flashbulbs were going off. Reporters from Channels 3 and 5 were already standing outside the home on the other side of the crime rope. Doug recognized Erin Wright and Linda McCullough from the TV stations.

"Can you tell us if the Neubauers are dead, Mr. Conrad? Paul, can you tell us what happened inside the home? Was it Quinton Reed who broke into the home? How did Mr. Reed know you children were being harbored there? Was there a leak in the police department?" Doug knew the questions would be endless, but he himself didn't have any of the answers to their questions.

"No comment at this time," Doug replied. *"Please, my children have been through enough for one night. Give us some time, please."*

Two police officers were in the front seat of the car. Once Taylor, Paul, and Doug squeezed into the backseat, the car pulled out and headed for the hospital. As soon as they were down the road and away from the street lights, everything was quiet in the car. The car radio was on and the dispatcher was confirming Squad car 207 on its way to Summa, carrying the Conrad family as passengers.

"Mr. Conrad, if you can hear my voice, I'm Cheryl, one of the dispatchers with the department. Don't know if you can hear all of the cheers in the background, but our entire staff is elated that your family is safe. We were all pulling for you. Prayers have been answered, and we wish you the very best as you all recover from this horrible ordeal. God is good."

Tears were streaming down Doug's face. He tried to say "thank you," but he was unable to utter a sound due to the overwhelming emotion he was feeling. Did his children survive at the expense of Mitch and Elaine? He didn't know the answer to that yet, but apprehension was building inside him as he recalled seeing both of them in a pool of their blood. He felt afraid . . . very afraid, and it wasn't a feeling he was used to.

It was 1:45 a.m. and, fortunately, there were few people in the E.R. They took Paul and Taylor to separate exam rooms right away. The entire staff knew all about the Conrad crime story—who didn't know? It was on all the stations locally and nationally. It was a big story that had captured everyone's heart, especially the people of Akron. The ER staff had been informed of the night's events by police and had been waiting for the ambulances to arrive. Soon it would be a media frenzy in the waiting room but security was prepared to deal with that.

As soon as the ambulances arrived and pulled up to the double doors, their trauma teams were ready with specialists on hand. Mitch was rushed to the operating room as was Quinton. Elaine was getting a CT scan and had regained semi-consciousness though she was in shock and very much confused.

Everyone was abuzz in the E.R. This was one of the most exciting nights for the E.R. in a long time and everyone wanted to meet the Conrad children to offer their goodwill and support. Both Paul and Taylor had been examined by the resident doctors. Paul had a badly sprained wrist caused, most likely, from the force of the bat swing making contact with Quinton's head. Other than that and his frayed nerves, he appeared to be okay. A witness assistant was already there to help Paul deal with the trauma. Taylor was going to need help too. Everyone who met Paul and Taylor observed how mature and poised they were, especially considering what they'd had to live through these past five days. They were very polite but somewhat quiet and withdrawn, naturally. A policeman stood guard outside their exam rooms. Nothing else was going to happen to these kids!

CHAPTER 77

Jim and Holly Pascoe walked into the E.R. waiting room and immediately saw Doug sitting in a chair accompanied by Officers Preston and Parker. They were having a serious discussion when Doug looked up and saw them walking toward him.

Doug rose from his seat and Jim threw his big arms around him. Several tears trickled down Doug's cheeks.

"Doug, how are the kids?"

"I don't know, Jim. They have to be a mess emotionally. We're all nervous wrecks right now."

"How can we help, Doug?" asked Pastor Pascoe.

"Paul will need the most help, Jim. He hit Quinton with a bat three times. Reed's in the O.R. right now. All we know is he's alive, but we're not sure if he'll pull through. In lots of way, I hope he doesn't make it so we don't have to endure a trial, and yet I'm not so sure how Paul will deal with the fact he killed someone should Reed die, even if Reed provoked the attack and Paul was justified. Paul is a 'gentle giant,' Jim. He was always a fun loving kid, light hearted, trusting."

"May I go in and talk to him?"

"Sure, if the docs are done with him. They're wrapping his wrist. A witness assistant is with him also."

Jim spoke to the employee at the desk and identified himself and his purpose for being there. Doug turned in time to see Jim go back through the corridor. Holly also had gained consent to speak to Taylor and she, too, was walking back to the exam rooms. How could Doug thank them enough for always being there for his family?

Doug returned to his seat to resume his conversation with the two officers.

About an hour later, an E.R. doctor came out to update Doug and the officers. Mitch and Elaine's two sons and their wives had arrived and were sitting in a private cubicle being updated by another officer.

"Your kids are going to be fine, physically, Mr. Conrad. Considering what they've both been through, they are doing remarkably well. Both will most likely need a sedative tonight in order to get any sleep or rest. After that, they should be fine.

The Neubauer family was called up to hear the doctor's report on their parents surrounded by Sgt. Parker and Officer Preston as well as Doug. The one son had his arm around Doug but both sons were visibly shaken. Doug's heart went out to both the boys.

"Mrs. Neubauer just underwent a CT scan, which showed she has a serious concussion and a skull fracture. There doesn't seem to be a blood clot or any internal bleeding, fortunately. There was some swelling of the brain which will be treated with steroids but we couldn't see any intracerebral hemorrhaging. She's in shock, understandably, and pretty confused right now. We don't anticipate any problem, but she'll be observed for a day or so and once she's stable, she may go home.

"Mr. Neubauer is still in O.R. He has a shattered collar bone and rib and a punctured right lung. The bullet shattered his shoulder blade as well. He lost a lot of blood and has been given a blood transfusion. He'll probably be in the O.R. for at least another hour, according to the cardiothoracic surgeon. He'll be under heavy sedation for the next five or six hours and in I.C.U. for a couple of days, so I suggest you not plan on sticking around here all night. He won't be able to carry on a conversation for awhile.

"And how is Quinton Reed?" asked Officer Parker.

"He, too, is still in the operating room. He has a concussion for one. The neurosurgeon has removed a blood clot and has to remove the pressure off his brain. He has what we call cerebral edema, swelling of the brain due to forced trauma. There's a lot of swelling. If he survives that, then the orthopedic surgeon will go in to repair the upper humerus bone in his right arm. The left arm was also broken and has been set. He's in a coma right now. He could be unconscious for days, weeks, or even months, and when or if he comes out of it, he could have total amnesia or not. We just don't know. Barring any unforeseen complications, he has a pretty good chance of surviving, but it will be a long haul for him.

"He'll also need a plastic surgeon to repair one of his eye sockets. Right now our main concern is the swelling and stopping any internal bleeding. It's safe to say Mr. Reed won't be going anywhere for awhile," the doctor concluded.

"Doctor, are my children free to go home with me now?" asked Doug.

"Yes, Mr. Conrad. As I said, the sedatives will settle them down tonight, so I recommend they both take them. Tomorrow they should feel well rested and ready to face whatever the day brings. Mr. Conrad, may I personally offer my condolences to you and your family for the loss of your wife. What's happened to you and your family has been heinous."

"I appreciate that, Doctor."

"Paul is in Room 4 and Taylor in Room 5, sir," directed the resident.

Doug walked back to their rooms and heard Jim praying the sweetest prayer for Paul. They were embraced. Paul had let every emotion go and looked like a little boy again, thought Doug. It broke his heart to see Paul so torn.

When he peeked inside Room 5, he heard Holly finishing up a prayer. Taylor gave her the most affectionate hug, and they continued to hold on to each other. It was the way he remembered Taylor hugging her mother.

Doug pulled the curtains back.

"Paul, Taylor, if you're ready, we'll go home. We've done all we can do here tonight." said Doug tenderly and affectionately.

Both Paul and Taylor hopped off their exam table, hugged Pastor and Mrs. Pascoe one more time and walked to Doug's loving arms.

"Let's go home, Dad. Let's go home."

CHAPTER 78

Allen Stanwick listened to the news on the radio in disbelief. While he was glad that the Conrad family had survived their ordeal, he was troubled that Quinton Reed had also, although it sounded like the Conrad boy had done some pretty serious damage to him. Too bad he hadn't killed him. That would have solved all of Allen's problems. If Quinton Reed lived long enough to talk to anyone, it could be all over for Allen. The authorities might get the proof they needed to arrest him for the murders of his client and her caregiver. The ramblings of a dying criminal might not be worth a whole lot, but if Quinton could direct them to his destroyed gun, forensics might be able to restore enough DNA to nail him.

He needed to make that issue go away. The police would be guarding him and would interrogate him as soon as he was alert enough to answer questions. Let's hope that never happened, thought Allen. Now that he was caught, Quinton would want to make a deal with the authorities.

CHAPTER 79

The day had come that Doug dreaded. Viewing hours. It was nearing the time when he would be saying goodbye to Cynthia forever. It was hard to fathom. Five days prior she was so full of life and dreams.

Hundreds of people streamed inside Grace Bible Church to pay their respect to Cynthia. People from their church were there in support as well as their neighbors, relatives, and a concerned public. All needed to express their sympathy in one way or another. Reporters and photographers were denied access inside but Doug didn't mind their being outside to film and record the tribute to Cynthia. Police were positioned inside and outside of the church to regulate the crowd and to keep their eyes open should the Conrad's still need protection. The facts and players of this heinous crime had not been completely sorted, and the authorities weren't 100 % sure that only one person was involved, so precautions were still going to be taken.

The family, naturally, had asked that their privacy be respected as they lay their loved one to rest. Many heart-warming moments provoked tears and caused pride to well up inside Doug, Paul, and Taylor as they heard so many stories of Cynthia's acts of kindness. The expressions of love for their family and for Cynthia was emotionally stirring. There were endless tears, hugs, kisses, and well wishes from their many friends and acquaintances as well as total strangers who for whatever reason felt compelled to lift their family up.

Before the doors were opened to the public, the immediate family had an hour to spend alone with Cynthia. She looked beautiful in her pink floral dress surrounded by a spray of pink and cream colored roses, baby pink carnations and pink gerber daisies with baby's breath and delicate white daisies. She looked so feminine. The room overflowed with well over one hundred floral arrangements of every type and kind. As they read the name tags, many were from people around the country whom they didn't even know who were expressing their heartfelt sympathy. Sweet notes and messages were attached that would have to be read later. It was overwhelming. Cynthia wouldn't have ever imagined such a thing.

The family had asked that in lieu of flowers, people send a donation to some of Cynthia's favorite charities—the battered women's shelter, Haven of Rest for the homeless, Akron Children's Hospital, children's medical research, and, of course, the Mission's Fund that would help *"spread the gospel to those who have not heard,"* as Cynthia would say. *"We need to feed their bellies, but also feed their souls."*

As the scheduled viewing hours were coming to a close, they had to be extended as the crowd continued to grow. There wasn't a dry eye in the church. It was obvious no one would have wanted to go through what the Conrad family had, but the community, Akron's mayor, even the state governor came to pay tribute to Cynthia.

Doug was impressed to have met the governor and his wife. His presence seemed humble and sincere and non-political.

"The entire state of Ohio stands behind you, Mr. Conrad. If there's anything I or my staff can do for you, please feel free to call." And with that, he handed Doug his business card which he tucked in his jacket pocket.

The mayor of Akron then stepped up, but there was something sheepish or demure about Mayor Stanwick's demeanor.

"I'm so sorry for the unnecessary pain you and your family have gone through, Doug. Thank goodness there is now closure to all of this."

Doug couldn't help but notice how quick the mayor was to assume the case was now closed. He also didn't offer support from the city or offer future help, which Doug found rather odd. Without giving Doug a chance to speak, the mayor stepped away as though deep in thought. Something was weighing heavy on his mind, and Doug knew that this case may not be as closed as the mayor thought it was. He himself had some lingering questions for the mayor, which centered around the early release of Quinton Reed.

Doug continued to greet people and looked up just as Mayor Stanwick was walking out of the sanctuary. The mayor turned back momentarily and their eyes locked.

Doug needed more time to process the mayor's comments. Something just wasn't feeling right, but it would come to him. It would.

CHAPTER 80

Doug could not put into words his gratitude for the love and concern that was expressed during this very long evening. After everyone had left, Doug stood for a long time looking at Cynthia, talking to her under his breath. Paul and Taylor stood back waiting for their father, giving him that precious private moment he needed. He reached over and kissed her goodnight. His chin was quivering and he looked exhausted as he walked towards his children to go home.

When they turned onto their road, their entire yard was lit up by people holding candles and a vigil. Their yard was filled with teddy bears of every size and kind and more flowers. Most faces they recognized as being their neighbors. They felt the love despite their feeling of desolation. Certainly, no man is an island. Doug and the kids were so spent, they had nothing more to give to anyone. They waved and said thank you audibly and bade the crowd goodnight.

A police car was at the curb in front of their house, reminding them of the circumstances that brought them to this day. One by one the candles were blown out in reverence and the crowd dissipated.

Doug, Paul, and Taylor sat in their warm, inviting kitchen looking at all of the food sitting on the counter and stuffed in their refrigerator supplied by neighbors and dear friends. They drank ice tea and discussed their reactions to the evening, reminiscing about the many discussions and comments made by their many friends, family, and acquaintances.

Some of those comments incited laughter. Some shared sweet or tender moments they had had with Cynthia. More tears as pride welled up in them. For sure, Mom was quite a woman and had made her mark on everyone who ever knew her. It was so hard to believe she was gone . . . forever. She died too soon.

Tomorrow would be the hardest day of their life and they were all feeling emotionally and physically exhausted. Doug gathered his kids together like a hen gathers her chicks and offered them a family hug.

"Try to get some sleep tonight. We all need to be rested for tomorrow."

Doug closed his bedroom door—the room he had shared for almost twenty five years with Cynthia, and the memories overwhelmed him. He saw her perfumes on the dresser and could almost smell her. He opened the top drawer of her dresser and saw her lipsticks all lined up, remembering how he used to watch her primp. The kisses and playful flirtations that took place in this room could fill a book. The intimacy. The serious yet warm and comfortable conversations they had would never take place again. Plans were made in this room. Sitting in the Jacuzzi together just relaxing together was now a thing of the past, and all because of one man. It was unbearable.

Snuggles was asleep on her back, stretched out on Cynthia's bed pillow. She was the perfect picture of tranquility and vulnerability. She was their beloved dog, but she was really Cynthia's dog. Snuggles would come to really miss her as Cynthia was so attentive to her needs and habits.

"Oh, God. What do I do now? Why, Lord? Please tell me, why? I almost lost my entire family this week. Thank you that I only lost one, but she was my soul mate. The love of my life. Help me to understand this, Lord, for I don't right now. I feel so alone and empty and angry."

Snuggles woke up and walked over to Doug who was sitting on the edge of the bed. She crawled on to his lap and stared into his eyes as though she understood every thing he had just whispered aloud. She licked his cheek with her bright pink, wet tongue and felt so warm and soft as he caressed her. Somehow Snuggles brought him a feeling of comfort he hadn't felt in days.

Tomorrow would be his worst day ever. He knew he needed to be strong for the sake of his children, but he didn't know how he was going to do that.

CHAPTER 81

P astor Pascoe bent over Doug and whispered something to him before climbing the three steps to his pulpit. Doug nodded in assent. The first ten rows of the sanctuary were comprised of Cynthia's and Doug's parents, the siblings, and nieces and nephews. Of course, Lucille and John Rogers and Holly Pascoe were part of the family.

Doug looked back and saw Mitch and Elaine's two sons sitting in the back. Hopefully, this meant that Mitch and Elaine were improving enough they felt comfortable to step away from them to attend the funeral.

The sanctuary which held 350 people was filled, and some chairs had been set down in the back and side aisles to accommodate some late comers.

Pastor Pascoe began the service in prayer and read some Bible scriptures that provided hope and assurance of life after death. Judy, a favorite church soloist stood up and began to sing *No More Night:*

The timeless theme, Earth and Heaven will pass away . . . evil is banished to eternal hell . . .

No more night, no more pain, no more tears never crying again . . . we will live in the light of the Risen Lamb.

It brought comfort to Doug. Behind him, he heard Cynthia's parents sobbing and watched his own kids wipe the tears streaming down their cheeks. The song was followed by Jim's reading of Revelations 21: 1-7,

Cynthia's favorite Bible passage. Jim moved into the more personal contributions and persona of Cynthia's life. He named specific things she did that meant so much to the family and to the church and what a wonderful Christian she truly was, and yet how humble she was. Jim talked about *"how deep the Father's love was for all of us, that our guilt was on His shoulders and that His wounds paid our ransom."*

Doug's anger toward Quinton Reed began to take on a different perspective. Pastor Pascoe continued . . ."*It was my sin that put Him there until it was accomplished. His dying breath has brought me life, I know that it is finished. God gave His only Son to make a wretch His treasure."*

Judy stood up again and sang another of Cynthia's favorite songs.

"We shall behold Him, face to face in all His glory . . . the sky shall unfold preparing His entrance, the stars shall applaud Him, as we behold Him face to face."

The funeral was victorious just as Cynthia would have wanted it. One by one the people in each pew walked by her casket for one more last look and final goodbye. Some lingered as though hanging on to a memory, some touched her hand or put their hand on her cheek. As the sanctuary emptied, the people returned to their cars to line up for the ride to the cemetery.

It was now time for the immediate family to bid their wife, mother, daughter, or sibling a final farewell. If Quinton Reed could have known the pain and sadness he invoked upon this family, would he have still murdered Cynthia in cold blood? Did he have no heart? Of course, if he could shoot his own son, why would he have any inhibitions to shoot a lady whom he really didn't know? Somehow Doug knew he was going to have to forgive Quinton Reed for murdering his wife. He had to rid himself of this anger and bitterness if he was to move on. He would think about that issue later.

As he and his children rose from the front pew, embracing one another, they stood in front of Cynthia and ten thousand memories rushed through Doug's mind. He couldn't take his eyes off his beautiful wife. Both Taylor and Paul kissed their mother and stepped away sobbing.

211

Doug took her hand and held it tenderly and bent over and kissed her hand. His hand slid up to her shoulders as though to embrace her and then as he kissed her on the lips one final time, he began to sob uncontrollably.

"I love you, Cynthia. I love you so much! You were the love of my life too! I promise I will protect our kids forever, sweetheart."

Their dad pulled something out of his pocket that looked like a plastic sandwich bag. Doug had the pendant in it that he gave to Cynthia when he first realized he loved her. It said *I promise to love you always* on the back of it. He had put an RSVP in it to her sandwich bag note: *You were the story of my life. It started the day we met and ends today. Much too soon. I am the one who owed you so much. Thank you for giving me our beautiful children. I will love them always for the both of us. Until we meet again, I will always love you."* He tucked the bag underneath her hands.

Paul stepped forward to put his arms around his Dad and led him to the limousine waiting to take them to Greenlawn Cemetery where Cynthia would be laid to rest. Reporters and photographers were outside capturing the magnitude of the moment. Over fifty cars were in the line up to go to the cemetery. It required police on motorcycles and a squad car to direct the motorcade.

As this was to be Cynthia's final earthly destination, Pastor Pascoe again offered hope and assurances of eternal life after death for believers. He also implored those present to find forgiveness in their hearts toward those who caused this pain so that *"our days might be more rewarding and we can find peace within."* Doug knew Jim was talking directly to him. There was no more that could be done for Cynthia, but there was plenty of issues in Doug's heart that needed attention.

After the pastor's final prayer, a few people placed a rose on top of Cynthia's casket. Others returned to their cars in silence while others made their way to the Conrads to offer their condolences one last time.

It was a beautiful, sunny day and an uplifting service that honored both Cynthia and God. Cynthia would have been pleased. Doug glanced once more at the graveside, gently placed the last rose on her casket and without looking back returned to the limo.

When they returned to the church, the family went to the church's dining room for a dinner prepared by the ladies of the church for the Conrad family and closest friends. As soon as they had eaten and thanked the cooks and servers, Doug went to his car. He had some important stops to make before the sun went down. He needed to check on Elaine and Mitch. As heavy as his heart was, he owed these two friends so much. He could never repay them for laying their very lives down to protect his kids, but he planned to be there for them every step of the way.

CHAPTER 82

ONE WEEK LATER

As soon as the resident doctor realized Quinton was awakening from his coma, the staff doctor informed Sgt. Parker as he was instructed to do. Officer Preston was sent to Summa Hospital within the hour to question Quinton.

Meanwhile, Dr. Acus, an orthopedic surgeon entered Quinton's room and explained that his left arm had been broken and already set but that he would be operated on tomorrow morning to repair his right humerus bone and upper shoulder. If everything went well, he would probably be released from the hospital several days later to the care of the Summit County Jail physician to recover. Dr. Acus was very professional, explained the procedure, asked if Quinton had any questions, and then left the room. There were no open signs of animosity or disgust. No signs of being judgmental, and yet Quinton assumed all of his caretakers knew what he had "*allegedly*" done. In fact, they had actually treated him with respect. Taking a hostage in order to escape would not be out of the question for him, but he would wait until he received all of his free medical care and then, if necessary, make a move if it was at all feasible. He needed to observe who the weakest, most vulnerable worker was who could play into his plan.

Quinton was aware of Officer Preston's entrance into his room and the purpose of his being there. He was somewhat groggy but exaggerated his grogginess and confusion to convince Officer Preston that it was still a little too early to press the suspect for information. Quinton needed more time to think of his responses that would work to his favor in a court of law, so he had no intentions of shooting off his mouth or saying anything that might compound his already gargantuan legal problems.

Not wanting to make his visit to the hospital a total waste, Officer Preston decided to give Quinton something to think about after he walked away.

"We know you killed Cynthia Conrad and a hunter by the name of Brady Randolph. You also had your son abduct Taylor Conrad. We believe you also intended to kill her but failed in that attempt. That led to your shooting your son, Kevin, who by the way is now in fair condition at Camden-Clark Memorial Hospital in Parkersburg, West Virginia.

"But not one to fail, Mr. Reed, you continued to heave vengeance on the Conrad family and invade a detective's home in order to kill both Taylor and Paul Conrad. However, your plan went awry and you ended up shooting a policeman and seriously assaulting his wife. Then you attempted to murder Paul and Taylor, but they got you instead. How are those for the facts we can prove in court, Quinton?"

"So what I'm saying is, we have to get you well, and then you're going down. You are never going to hurt or terrorize anyone ever again."

Quinton's eyes remained closed the entire time and he pretended not to hear a thing. The cops knew pretty much everything, but Quinton still felt like he had a bargaining chip he could use. He just wasn't ready to use it, and he needed more time when he could think clearer and figure out a strategy for working a deal.

His best way out would be to escape, but he knew an armed cop was sitting outside his room and that he was cuffed to the bed slats, so an escape was unlikely if not totally impossible.

CHAPTER 83

Quinton had spent the last three hours in recovery and was being returned to his private room that would be heavily guarded. Again, he was cuffed to the bed. Quinton was in a cast all the way up to his shoulder and had his upper torso wrapped securely. As weak and groggy as he was, he was still contemplating how he could escape the hospital or work a deal to receive a lighter sentence, escaping the death penalty. He believed he had valuable information that could keep him from lethal injection, but if the cop he shot died, it would surely be voided. He thought of how he could spin his story of the last five days but forensics would be able to prove him a liar. They would be in possession of his Judge and be able to match the bullets that killed the victims to his gun. There was absolutely no way to escape imprisonment for life unless he could work out a deal or if he escaped. In his present condition, escape was unlikely, but perhaps not impossible . . . with help.

CHAPTER 84

The morning after his surgery, Quinton was much more alert. Dr. Acus had come in and discussed the surgery with him and the range of movement he could expect to have with the arm after several months. He would need physical therapy but wasn't sure what would be available to him. Quinton smirked, knowing he was screwed and would pretty much be on his own to work on it by himself.

Nurses had come in throughout the night and early morning hours to check his vital signs or to check his IV. A young male worker named Fred assisted him onto his bed pan. He seemed like a free-spirit. His hair was in a pony-tail past his shoulders and he had a short beard and unkempt mustache. He knew every employee who entered his room was aware of who he was and all what he had done. He was also sure they were warned not to fraternize with him or to get too close.

People, however, love to act like they have first hand knowledge of someone like him. It makes for not only a great story, but it gives them a sense of importance as they share the conversations they exchanged with him. The females were extra cautious when they entered his room. Oftentimes the guard sitting outside would step just inside the door to offer them a sense of safety. But Fred seemed relaxed when he entered.

Quinton knew he would have to work a ruse on Fred quickly before he was to be transferred to the Summit County Jail's Infirmary. He began having casual conversations with him, finding out things about Fred's personal life. Fred was 21 years old and had worked at the hospital for only four months. He had a girlfriend that he was hoping to make his bride, but he hadn't popped the question yet. Quinton saw a bulge in his back pocket that looked like a cell phone.

"I know I've blown my life pretty much. I was sucked into committing these crimes for someone else. I guess you could say, 'I was bought with a price.' Well, it's too late for me, but I have a girlfriend I'd like to at least talk to before I'm sent off to Sing Sing. Wonder if you'd let me borrow your cell phone and let me talk to her for just a few minutes. Alone."

Fred looked sheepish and indecisive. He glanced back at the door as though he should first ask the guard.

"I just need 5 minutes to tell her I love her. Surely you can understand that."

"I guess there's no harm in that. You want me to dial her number for you?"

"No, I think I can manage with my left hand. I'll be quick. Give me 5 minutes alone, and you can come back in and get your phone." He pulled his cuffed ankle up as far as the cuffs would allow. *"As you can see, I'm not going anywhere,"* Quinton replied.

Fred still looked hesitant and then pulled his cell phone out of his pocket and handed it to Quinton. Reticently he commented,

"Listen, dude, I've only worked here for four months. I can't afford to lose my job, so make it quick. I'll be back in 5 minutes."

As soon as Fred stepped out of the room and closed the door, Quinton dialed up a number he had memorized. As soon as he heard a pick up at the other end and recognized the reluctant hello, he heard,

> *"Why are you calling me?"*
> *"I have 5 minutes so listen up. I'm cuffed to my bed in Room 350 with a cop outside my room. I either need your help for a timely escape OR I'll have to make a plea bargain deal with the prosecutors."*

"And why would they make a deal with you at this point? They have too much proof against you."

"True, but I have some information on you that they would be very interested in."

"You don't have anything on me. And, for sure, now, you don't have any proof."

"Well, my friend, that's where you're wrong. I forgot to tell you but I decided at the last minute not to destroy your gun. I figured it was my 'Get out of Jail' card should I ever need it. I'm not sure why you wanted it destroyed, but I figured the cops could figure it out once they got their hands on it. If you got Mr. Mayor to get me out of prison two months early, it must have been pretty urgent. We'll just let the cops sort through it all. I'm sure the $50,000 is a paper trail that would lead back to you as well. I have nothing to lose, so if you want to negotiate with me, do it fast. I swear I will tell the cops where to find your gun IF you don't get me out of here."

"You lying, double crosser! After I got you out of prison, gave you $50,000 for doing nothing more than destroying my gun and clothes, you destroyed your life, my life, and the Conrad family. You could have moved on, had a decent life. I don't get it. Why? Why didn't you follow the plan?" asked Allen.

"No time for why's, bro. Get Uncle Mayor to help if need be. You get me far away from here, and I promise, I will get lost forever and never speak your name again. I will also tell you where your gun is hidden so all bribes end."

"All right, I'll see what I can do, but it won't —"

"Remember, honey, I love you and depend on your support, no matter what happens. Bye for now!" Click.

Fred walked into the room and saw Quinton end the call. He had latex gloves on his hands and quickly took his phone and returned it to his back pocket.

"Thanks, good Buddy!" Quinton said with a smirk and a wink.

"No problem," responded Fred. He emptied Quinton's bed pan and quickly left the room.

CHAPTER 85

Sgt. Parker, Officer Preston, Dr. Brandon White, a psychologist and criminal profiler, Bob Welch, an undercover cop better known as *"Fred,"* and Doug Conrad sat around a conference table and listened.

" . . . I either need your help for a timely escape OR I'll have to make a plea bargain with the prosecutors."

"And why would they make a deal with you at this point? They have too much proof against you."

"True, but I have some information on you that they would be very interested in."

"You don't have anything on me. And, for sure, now you don't have any proof."

All four of them listened in total disbelief. The clarity of this conversation and the information revealed in it was priceless. It was putting everything into perspective for the authorities and helped them dot their *I's* in this case.

" . . . I swear I will tell the cops where to find your gun IF you don't get me out of here . . ."

"You lying double crosser! After I got you out of prison, gave you $50,000 for doing nothing more than destroying my gun and clothes, you destroyed your life, my life, and the Conrad family . . . I don't get it. Why didn't you follow the plan?"

It was clearly Allen Stanwick's voice. The phone number was verified. With the facts that they had already collected, it was becoming clearer what the connection was between Allen Stanwick, the Mayor, and Quinton Reed.

Dr. White was pretty certain that once confronted with their proof, Quinton Reed would confess and tell all. Quinton wasn't the typical cold blooded killer, but he was a narcissist who believed in holding a grudge and punishing the person whom he felt wronged him. He was unforgiving, and anyone who interfered with his plan to get even was dealt with. All throughout his life he had tried talking his way out of trouble to avoid punishment, and in the legal system, it had even worked for him once or twice. But now Reed had to know he was beyond the point of no return. He would never again be a free man and could even receive the death penalty. His only recourse was to assist the police in solving another case that he had ironically and somewhat innocently become an accessory to. If he cooperated and helped bring the McGrary /Stover case to closure, then the State would most likely give Reed life.

CHAPTER 86

Doug hugged both of his children this morning as they pulled out of the driveway to return to their universities and resume their lives. It would be the best thing for his kids—delve into their studies, get back into campus activities, and return to their friends. He knew their grades might suffer this semester, but right now their mental health was so much more important to him.

As he walked up his driveway, he heard a car pull up to the curb. He paused to see who it was. A woman whom he didn't recognize quickly got out of the car and called out his name.

He thought it was probably a reporter and he had no desire to talk to her or anyone, for that matter.

"Mr. Conrad! Please. I need to talk to you. It's very important!" She seemed quite stressed.

He stopped to allow her time to come up the driveway to him. He didn't recognize her car, but now that she got closer, there was something about her demeanor that seemed familiar. She appeared very nervous and emotional.

"I'm so sorry to bother you right now. In fact, I'm probably one of the last people you'd like to talk to, but I don't know who to turn to. Before I tell you who I am, please promise me you'll give me just five minutes of your time. Please."

The strain in her face was evident and it took little deduction to see the woman was on the verge of falling to pieces. Tears were welling up in her eyes already.

"Very well. I'm listening."

"My name is Ramona Reed, the ex-wife of Quinton but the proud mother of Kevin."

Doug realized he had been to her home over fifteen years ago when her children were just toddlers. He now realized why her face looked somewhat familiar.

"I am so, so sorry for your great loss, and I'm so sorry for my son's role in your daughter's abduction. I beg for your forgiveness, on my son's behalf." Her voice was almost inaudible as tears poured down her cheeks.

"Mrs. Reed, why don't we walk to the back patio where we can have a private conversation."

"Thank you, Mr. Conrad."

"Doug, please. May I call you Ramona?"

"That would be fine."

"So how is your son, Kevin?"

"He was released from the hospital and is sitting in the Parkersburg jail. I know he's in a lot of trouble. By crossing state lines with Taylor, he's committed a federal crime and they're pouring on the charges, including accessory to murder. But that's not why I'm here.

"I guess the most important thing I want you to know is that my son is a good boy. Until September tenth, he never had any kind of a criminal record, not even a traffic ticket. He was raised without a father and never caused me an ounce of trouble while growing up. He was a B/C student in school and was active in sports. She paused, choking back tears. *We didn't have a lot of extra money, but Kevin had a part-time job while in high school to help me out. He was a loving, respectful son, and he was always loved. He knew I loved him.*

"I worked hard trying to support three sons by myself. It wasn't easy from a financial standpoint. My boys didn't have all the fancy clothes and things that other kids had, but we got by."

Doug listened attentively as Ramona continued on. He saw her sincerity and her need to get this off her chest.

"I didn't know how much my son needed a father. I swear to you, none of us knew Quinton was released early from prison. Neither I nor my other two sons knew that Kevin had any verbal contact with Quinton, much less that he had met him after he was released.

"My son's biggest mistake was being gullible. I never bad mouthed their father. I saw no purpose in that. They knew he was in prison and they knew why he was there. I let them put the dots together. I certainly didn't extol him either so that they would want to have a relationship with him. Maybe I should have described what he was like in more disparaging terms when we were a family, but I just thought, 'out of sight, out of mind.' I miscalculated their needs . . . well, Kevin's anyways.

"Kevin's motive for taking Taylor was to please his father and have an opportunity to meet him and build a relationship with him. Quinton fed him lies, promising that neither Taylor nor her mother would be hurt. In fact, Kevin thought they were going to be detained for several days and then freed unharmed.

"When Kevin arrived at the designated location and realized it was all a lie, he should have gotten back in the car with Taylor and taken off. But, he made sure Taylor at least got away. He felt duped. He wanted to confront his dad and demand the truth. He wanted to believe the best about Quinton, but as you know, Quinton shot and nearly killed him. Tears were streaming down her cheeks.

"It was important to me that you hear what really happened. My son told me and the F.B.I. everything about that night. His story supports the evidence.

"So he never intended to harm your daughter, even though he ended up scaring her and sedating her. Those were Quinton's strong directives. He took advantage of a young kid who so wanted to please his father and help him out.

"My son has been demonized by the press, and it hurts my soul because I know Kevin's heart. If Quinton lives, he has a lot to answer

for. Kevin is so very sorry. He wanted Taylor to know he never meant to harm her."

"I do thank you for sharing this information, even though you shouldn't be talking to me now, Ramona. As a parent, however, I understand your need to explain.

"I'm sure at trial these facts will all come out and the courts will probably show as much mercy on Kevin as allowed. It will certainly be a teachable moment for him. It was an evening for many regrets."

"Yes, it was. I'm sorry I ever knew Quinton, and my boys feel so betrayed and humiliated by their father. We've all been victimized by him—you more than us, we know."

"Yes, we have," was all Doug could say to that.

"Well, I need to be going. I know I shouldn't have come—for all the legal reasons—but for personal reasons, I needed to express my condolences to you and beg for your forgiveness. I'm not asking for anything from you, but that you understand the background."

"Thank you, Ramona. I do appreciate that. I will share this conversation with Taylor. While she was put directly in harm's way by Kevin, she also knows he saved her life that night, and for that we are all forever grateful."

"Me, too, Mr. Conrad. I need to go now." She got up, surprised him with a hug, and turned and left.

Doug watched her leave. The lady took a huge risk by coming here. She didn't know what kind of a reception she would get, but she followed her heart and conscience. The lawyers would say she should have stayed away, but Doug actually felt better because she did come. In his heart, it made a difference.

CHAPTER 87

The F.B.I., Parkersburg police, and the APD had been pooling the information gathered from their investigations and were getting a clearer picture of each suspect's role in the Conrad case.

Much information had been gleaned from Kevin Reed. He was a very naïve and vulnerable kid—actually a good kid—who was led astray by a father whom he so desperately wanted to meet.

The Akron police had spoken to Kevin's high school teachers, counselors, and administrators to get a clearer profile of this young man. His attendance and discipline record throughout all four years of school were untarnished. All of the teachers questioned said he was pleasant and very polite in class. He was a *"people pleaser."* All of the staff were baffled when they learned of his role in the Conrad case—they were in disbelief. It was *"so out of character"* for Kevin.

While there was great sympathy for this boy, the law still couldn't condone him for his willing participation in abducting and chloroforming the Conrad girl. Conceivably, he could have killed her. He took her across state lines not realizing that that in itself escalated the charges and his legal problems. Nor did that excuse his not going straight to the police when he first learned who had abducted Cynthia Conrad and even knew how to find her, knowing that authorities had been searching for her. Perhaps her life could have been saved if he had come forward.

However, the psychologist discussed his *"childlike faith in his father"* despite knowing his dad was a felon.

Kevin truly believed his father was following a plan that would kick start his new life as a free man. Kevin believed he would have some role in that life. And he firmly believed his father had no plans to harm Taylor nor Cynthia Conrad until he arrived in the woods that night and witnessed the chaotic situation playing out right then.

Kevin willingly took a polygraph test and was given a psychological test. He passed both. He spoke freely with the police even after being read the Miranda rites. Once his mother hired a criminal lawyer to represent her son, Kevin was silenced. The authorities, however, had already heard his testimony about everything that had happened on September 10 . The valuable information obtained from Kevin directed their follow-up investigation.

CHAPTER 88

Quinton Reed's stolen car had been impounded and the bag of $50,000 found. Thanks to Reed's phone conversation, it would be much easier to track the source of the money.

The Conrad case was pointing them toward another unsolved case in Summit County. There was clearly a link to these two cases, and it was becoming clearer by the hour.

The troubling aspect was it was leading them straight to the mayor's doorstep and to his nephew. This would be devastating to the stability of the city and very disconcerting to the people of Akron who strongly supported the city's leadership.

Sgt. Parker, Officer Preston, and the F.B.I. felt these cases would be coming to a fast conclusion within the next couple of days as their suspicions were being confirmed and test results came back from forensics. Reed had all the answers to their questions. It was now time to revisit him at Summa Hospital.

As Sgt. Parker was sitting in his office ready to leave, his office phone rang. Quinton Reed was asking to see his lawyer, but not just any lawyer. He wanted Allen Stanwick.

CHAPTER 89

Susan Stanwick knew her husband was a busy lawyer, and since his suspicion for the murders of Mrs. McGrary and Madeline Stover, he had been under undue stress. She knew her husband, and while he was sometimes haughty, self-serving, and dominating, he was, nevertheless, a good man. He was a dauntless lawyer in the courtroom, always fighting for the rights of his clients. She loved her father whose law firm Allen worked for, but she felt a certain amount of resentment towards him because he had refused to make Allen a partner in the practice. However, she had never had enough nerve to ask her father his specific reasons for denying Allen partnership.

Allen had been so preoccupied lately and irascible that she and Tommy, their nine year old son, had given him his space and made little demands on him. As soon as the dark cloud of suspicion cleared regarding these two murders, Allen would bounce back. Of that she was sure.

He had not come home from the office until after 10:30 p.m. He was trying to close some of his cases and organize some of his client files. When he came home, she heard him go into Tommy's bedroom to kiss him goodnight. Tommy must have awakened because she heard them talking and laughing. Tommy seemed so happy. Allen had not spent much time with Tommy or her for a very long time. Allen seemed at peace and contented when he stepped into their bedroom.

Allen gave her a very passionate kiss and sat in a chair nearest her side of the bed.

"I've taken the first half of the morning off tomorrow, Susan. I want to work in the study the first half of the morning and organize some of our personal business. I thought maybe I could take you to lunch tomorrow and then go into the office. How about if we go to Ken Stewart's for lunch?"

Ken Stewart's Grille was one of Akron's best fine dining restaurants. He knew Susan particularly loved it. He took clients there frequently but never Susan.

"Wow! It's not even my birthday! I can't think of the last time we had lunch together. That would be wonderful, darling! I'd love that, but what's the occasion?"

"No occasion. We haven't spent much time together, and I just wanted to have some alone time with you since Tommy's back in school."

His countenance changed from happy to serious.

"Susan?"

"What, hon?"

"Do you love me?"

"What kind of question is that? You know I love you."

"I love you too, Susan. I've never really told you this before, but I appreciate how you've raised Tommy. I know I've had very little to do with that. He's such a good boy. I've been too engaged at the office, and I know I've neglected you both, and for that I'm truly sorry."

"Why so serious, Allen? Why now?"

"I guess I'm just being introspective. I see myself as having been selfish. I . . ."

"How can you say that Allen? You've provided us with such a beautiful home. I drive a BMW. Tommy has everything he could possibly want. You've been very generous to us. You work hard and work such long hours just so we can have these nice things. Having grown up with a father for a lawyer, I know how that is, but we do wish you were home more. Tommy needs you. I need you."

Allen still seemed pensive yet reticent.

"What's going on, Allen?"

"It's nothing, Susan. It's just when I look in the mirror, I don't like what I see. I see my foibles and frailties, and I know I'm unworthy of you and Tommy. I wanted the best for you, for Tommy, for the family."

" Oh, stop! We have the best, Allen!"

He stood up, leaned over and kissed her gently on the forehead.

"I don't deserve you."

He walked to the walk-in closet and tossed his tie over a hanger and then hung up his suit. As she watched him remove his clothes, she couldn't help but admire his muscular thighs and biceps. His hairy chest and legs had always been a turn on for her. He seemed to get sexier with age. He walked naked to the bathroom and showered. He stepped out of the master bathroom holding his pajama bottoms in hand and dropped them on the floor beside his side of the bed. He slipped between the sheets and before she could say *please* he had her nightgown off and they were making love. He had never been this hungry or passionate, not even on their honeymoon night.

Whatever was going on, she liked it.

CHAPTER 90

Allen had taken his morning cup of coffee into the study and closed the door behind him. He had been in there working quietly all morning. She wasn't sure what he was doing, but she knew he didn't want to be disturbed.

Their reservation for lunch was for noon. She had put on her blue twill stretch pants and a V neck form fitting top that made her look especially sexy. She pulled her long hair up and barretted it so that her long exotic earrings put the finishing touch to her exquisite appearance.

Allen held her hand as they walked into the restaurant. As the hostess led them to their table, he had his hand on the middle of her back in a very sensuous way. He even pulled her seat out for her. Allen hadn't been this attentive to her needs since they had dated. Whatever led to Allen's transformation, she liked it and hoped it would stay forever.

They shared an appetizer of crispy calamari and both ordered the jumbo lump crab cakes for lunch. They enjoyed a glass of white Zinfandel wine and finished with a berry shortcake for dessert, a Ken Stewart's favorite. It was a beautiful sunny day as they walked across the street to the parking lot.

Allen unlocked his sports car and kissed Susan on the cheek while handing her the outstretched seatbelt. They reminisced about fun times all the way home. He leaned over to kiss her as he dropped her off in front of their house. He lingered a little longer as he held onto her hand.

So what are you going to do the rest of the afternoon, wifey?" asked Allen.

"Well, since I'm having such a great day so far, I may just run to Summit Mall and do a little shopping before Tommy gets off the school bus."

"Actually, I thought I might pick Tommy up from school and maybe take him to Laser Quest and then to Dairy Queen for dinner. Would that be okay with you?"

"He'd love that Allen."

"I'll have him home by 7 p.m. in case he has any school work."

"Sounds like a great plan. Love you, sweetie."

"I love you too, Susan. More than you know."

CHAPTER 91

Allen made a quick call to Tommy's school while driving straight to his building. Tommy, looking rather inquisitively, was waiting in the office for his dad. Allen had called the school ahead and told them there was a family emergency and that Tommy would need to be pulled from school for just the afternoon. Not demanding an explanation for the emergency, the principal had Allen sign the Sign Out sheet, indicating the time, date, and reason for the withdrawal for school records.

As soon as Tommy got in the car, Allen announced they were going to the Cleveland Zoo and RainForest. Tommy, who was in the fourth grade, squealed with delight. He had been asking to visit the RainForest and zoo for months, but reasons were always given as to why they couldn't go.

"Tommy, I don't usually believe in fibbing to your school in order to play hooky like this, so this is the one and only time this will ever happen. It's just that today is a special day. I really need to talk to you and want to spend some time with you."

They talked about many different things as they drove north to Cleveland. Allen was in awe of his son's ability to carry on such a fun and lively conversation. He had certainly missed out on many father-son activities due to his work. He now regretted that.

Tommy was in awe of the rainforest, but he equally enjoyed the zoo. He stood for ten minutes admiring the lions and tigers. They moved on to the lemurs and Tommy was totally intrigued by their antics. As they stood in front of the gorilla cage, Allen said,

"How would you like to be caged like that, Tommy, when you could never get out for the rest of your life?"

"I wouldn't like it. I'd rather be dead," said Tommy.

"Me too. They were never meant to be caged. Like us, they need their freedom to be totally happy, don't they?"

"I'm sure they never meant to get caught," continued Tommy.

"I'm sure they didn't, Tommy. It's just like criminals, son. They do something wrong, and they think they'll never get caught. But then they make mistakes and they get cornered. The police arrest them, they go to trial, and then get sentenced to jail."

"Yeah, but they had a choice to do wrong, Dad. These animals weren't doing anything wrong but being animals when they got caught."

"True, son. Sometimes good guys make mistakes. Big mistakes. Then when they make the mistake, they don't know how to correct it, so they make even bigger mistakes in order to not get caught. They make bad choices."

"Well, they should go to the police and confess. Then maybe they wouldn't be punished. Sometimes if I do something wrong, I go to Mom and tell her, and she hugs me and forgives me."

"That works with mommies and daddies, son, but that doesn't work when you break the law. You're going to go to jail. And the worse the crime, the longer you go to jail."

"What if we opened up all of the animal cages and set the animals free, Dad?"

"What do you think would happen, Tommy?"

"Lots of people would get hurt, I suppose."

"You're right. So if we can't return them to the jungle where they came from, it's best to keep them caged."

"But if they're released, we would never get to see them again. Would we?"

"No, but the animals would be much happier, wouldn't they be?"

"Yes."

"So what would you prefer? To see them in a cage or know that they were set free and happy?"

"Well, I guess I would rather they be set free."

"Me too, Tommy."

They leisurely walked all around the zoo and ate a warm twist pretzel and pop and had the best time ever. Tommy looked so happy as they moved from one section to the next at the zoo. Allen had brought his digital camera and had asked visitors if they would mind taking their picture. They were getting hungry so they made their way to the Food Court and had a cheeseburger and fries.

On the way home, Tommy looked elated.

"This was the best day of my life, Dad! Thanks! We should do this again!"

"I'd like that son. I really would."

Allen pulled up in front of their house and let Tommy out.

"Tommy, I need to run an errand and won't be back for awhile. Tell your Mom not to expect me home this evening. Also, would you give this envelope to your mother just before you go to bed tonight?"

"What is it, Dad?"

"Just a little note I have for her. I don't want her to read it until after you go to bed. Can you do that for me, Tommy? It's a surprise for Mommy, so can you hide it from her until then?"

"Sure, Dad."

"Okay, son. Well, kiss me goodbye."

Allen put his arms around his son and never wanted to let go. There was such a strong physical resemblance between father and son. He hoped Tommy grew up to be a far better man than he.

"I love you so much, Tommy. I want you to know I am so proud of you. You're such a good boy, and I want you to always stay that way. I want you to give your best in life and always be honest and play life by the rules. Do you understand?"

"Sure, Dad."

"Love you, son, more than you'll ever know."

"I love you too, Dad."

Allen handed his son the digital camera to take into the house and watched his son enter the house safely before driving off. He saw Susan peaking out the window from around the curtain. She looked a bit surprised that he wasn't coming in. Allen turned his cell phone off and headed for downtown Akron.

CHAPTER 92

Allen stopped at a mailbox and tossed four envelopes into it. Last evening he had written four carefully yet succinct letters to Uncle Steve, his parents, Sgt. Parker, and Doug Conrad. This morning, he penned Tommy a letter and put it under his pillow. He had also written Susan a letter but put it inside the bottom folder on the desk in their study. She would find it soon.

It outlined for her directions for paying all of the house utilities and mortgage payments. All of their insurance policies which listed the beneficiaries were in another folder. The last folder was his will and testament, the trust, the living will, and funeral arrangements.

He couldn't figure out a way to shut Quinton Reed up without killing him and enough people had died already. There was no way he could redeem himself in the eyes of his family or the public. He was about to be disbarred and go to prison. There was no way for him to save face. He couldn't forgive himself much less ask his family or Doug Conrad to forgive him. His ruse to distract Doug Conrad had gone awry, and he was sure no one would ever believe that he meant no harm to Cynthia Conrad or to the Conrad family. He simply refused to live in a cell like a caged animal at the zoo, so there was only one way to escape that.

Allen turned west onto Tallmadge Avenue and turned left onto State Road where he parked his car near the Y-Bridge nicknamed "Suicide Bridge." Twenty-nine people had committed suicide since 1997 on it and now the city was investing $1.5 million to add fencing to prevent jumpers from making the plunge. He would be number 30. The bridge was suspended 134 feet above the Little Cuyahoga River. Allen walked halfway across the bridge as traffic moved swiftly alongside him. He looked over the railing and before anyone could figure out his intentions, he stepped over the railing and clung to it. Several quick observers started tooting their horns. A police car was just starting to drive across the bridge when he saw Allen.

A lady stopped her car and put her passenger window down.

"Whatever is the problem, Mister, it can be solved. You don't need to do this!"

Another man leaped out of his car and yelled, *"Please. Let me come to you. Let's talk, good buddy. Things are going to be okay."*

Allen saw the police officer drawing nearer.

"You're wrong about that. I can't right my wrongs. Greed was the root of my troubles and now I've hurt too many innocent people. I can't take any of it back, and I can't live with the guilt so it's too late for me."

Afraid that the man would lunge to grab him, Allen let go.

CHAPTER 93

Susan hugged Tommy as soon as he stepped inside the foyer.

"Where's Daddy going, Tommy?"

"He said he had to run an errand and wouldn't be home this evening."

That was odd, Susan thought. He never mentioned having to run an errand to her.

"So how was Laser Quest and Dairy Queen?"

"Dairy Queen?"

"Yeah. Didn't you eat dinner there this evening?"

"No. We ate at the Food Court at the zoo."

The Akron Zoo?"

"No, the Cleveland Zoo. We went to the RainForest too," responded Tommy with excitement.

"Didn't Daddy pick you up after school today?"

"No, he came earlier," Tommy said sheepishly.

Once he saw his Mom didn't know anything about that, he was afraid she might be mad, so he started to clam up.

"How much earlier?"

"I don't know."

She saw Tommy was feeling uncomfortable, so she decided to take another approach.

"So what did you like best at the zoo?"

Tommy's face lit up, and he began to describe all of the animals he had seen and the many different kinds of butterflies he saw in the RainForest.

Susan was delighted to see that Tommy had spent a day with his dad. That was well overdue, but it didn't explain why Allen did it on a school day rather than on a Saturday nor why he lied to her about his plans with Tommy. These plans had to be pre-calculated.

What was going on with Allen?

Tommy indicated he had some math homework, so after he completed it, she checked his answers. It was getting near bedtime, so she had him go upstairs and take a bath and get ready for bed. She laid out the clothes he would wear for tomorrow for school and made sure his book bag was organized. Tommy hopped into bed. He looked so adorable in his pajamas that had trains on them.

"Are you tired, honey?"

"Yes. That's a big zoo! I can't wait to go again. We had so much fun, Mommy!"

"I'm glad, son. Your daddy and I are so proud of you. You're such a good boy!"

"I know Mommy. Daddy said so too. You know what I'm going to do?"

"What?"

"I'm going to do my best and always play life by the rules."

"Is that what your father talked to you about today?"

"Yes."

"That's great advice, son. For all of us. I'm glad you had such a nice day with Daddy." She bent down and gave him a kiss and turned out the lights. Before she could say *"Sweet dreams"* Tommy spoke up.

"Oh, Mommy. Daddy wanted me to give you this when I went to bed tonight." He handed her an envelope with her name on it.

"Thanks, Tommy. See you in the morning."

"Goodnight, Mommy."

CHAPTER 94

A bad feeling was coming all over Susan. She couldn't explain it, but something just didn't feel right. She went downstairs and turned the TV on in their family room. It was just about time for *Criminal Minds* to start. She sat on the couch and tore the envelope open. It was clearly Allen's handwriting.

Dear Susan,

I had today carefully planned out. I wanted it to be a special and memorable day for us. A happy time as it will need to last a lifetime.

An ominous feeling was now coming over Susan as she continued to read.

The old cliché says, 'but all good things must come to an end' and how true that is.

By the time you get this note, I will be dead by my own doing. Please forgive me. You will understand after you read the letter I have for you in a folder in the study. I have detailed for you what precipitated my suicide. I have hurt everyone by my shameful behavior. I've lied to you and the authorities about the murders of Mrs. McGrary and Madeline Stover, so now I must be truthful. No more lies or hypocrisy. I have written letters to the APD and Doug Conrad detailing my roles and motives in these crimes. They should receive their letters tomorrow or Friday. Please forgive me.

Susan couldn't believe what she was reading. This letter scared her. Was he admitting to killing those two ladies? Her husband? Surely not! As she looked up at the TV, there was some breaking news.

"A man has just jumped off the Y-Bridge here in downtown Akron, but authorities haven't identified him yet. They believe he parked his 2009 Mazda MX-5 Miata on the side of the road near the bridge and walked to the center. Several passersby witnessed it and attempted to talk the well dressed gentleman out of jumping. The witnesses were so emotionally distraught they refused to talk to us. A police officer was at the scene also . . ."

Susan went completely deaf. She had heard enough. Having heard the description of the car, she knew who it was. Fear welled up in her and the tears were streaming down her cheeks. Today was all making sense to her now. How could she not have seen it? How could she have been so naïve?

She went straight to the study and saw the folders all lined up on the desk. When she got to the third folder, she saw the letter Allen was referring to. It was quite lengthy and he explained in great detail what happened inside Mrs. McGrary's home. He explained how Ramona Reed, a secretary in their law office, had an ex-husband who was in prison and having checked his record thought he could service him in hiding important evidence in his case, so he asked his Uncle Steve to request Quinton Reed's release from prison two months early. The early release was under the guise to help Ramona out as she struggled to raise three boys all by herself. Uncle Steve was being sucked into this ruse by deceit as well. A deal was worked out with Quinton, but Allen was double crossed by him. Not only had Allen deceived her with his lies and explanations, but he had deceived Uncle Steve and worse yet, used his power and influence to help Allen out. How do you compromise the reputation of an uncle who literally reared you for four years and had taken a special interest in your life since you were born? Uncle Steve had been wonderful to Allen, to her, and to Tommy. He loved them so much.

From this day forward, their lives would be changed. The shock was too much for her, but she needed help, and she needed it fast. Before she called her father, she called Uncle Steve.

CHAPTER 95

Steve Stanwick picked up the phone on the second ring. Having caller I.D., he knew it was Allen or Susan.

"Hello there!"

"Uncle Steve? Something terrible . . ." She was sobbing.

"Susan?"

"Something terrible has happened! I think Allen has committed suicide! Have you heard the breaking news?"

" What? How? Why? No, I haven't had the TV on all evening. Susan, talk to me."

She was crying so hard, he could hardly understand her.

"All I know is that someone jumped off the Y-Bridge, and I think it was Allen. He wrote me a letter. He wrote you one too. He acted strange today. I should have seen it, but I didn't. Please. Call the police. Find out who jumped off that bridge. Find Allen for me, please . . ."

"I'll call you as soon as I find out something. There has to be some mistake. Hang in there."

Steve hung up immediately and dialed the Police Chief. He would know in minutes who jumped off the bridge. While dialing the phone, he turned the TV on to see if he could hear the Breaking News.

CHAPTER 96

FIVE DAYS LATER

There was hardly a news station in Summit County or across the nation that hadn't covered the Conrad case. As more facts leaked out about this case from the investigation and recent suicide of Allen Stanwick, the case was being pursued by *60 Minutes* and *Time Line*. With greed and revenge as the motives, screenwriters were standing in line to turn this case into a Hollywood movie. There was money to be made on this case for sure.

For Quinton Reed, it meant his bargaining chip no longer existed. Once Sgt. Parker received and read his letter from Allen Stanwick himself and read those of Susan Stanwick, the mayor, and Doug Conrad, he was able to connect the dots in this case. The *how's* and *why's* were all coming together. His investigative team was checking the details presented by Allen Stanwick and Kevin Reed to verify how these two cases intertwined. And, of course, Quinton Reed was demanding the best public defender that money from the tax payers could buy. Public opinion was so strong, it was likely that Quinton Reed's trial would have to be held outside the district.

Steve Stanwick had been exonerated as an accomplice in this case, having been deceived by Allen. Obstruction of justice wasn't something the police wanted to pursue either although the mayor had sensed that Allen was hiding something from him. His love for his nephew allowed him to trust Allen and believe in his innocence in the McGrary and Stover case. More importantly, there was closure for the families of Harriet McGrary and Madeline Stover as well.

Kevin Reed's trial would most likely take place in a Summit County courtroom with Taylor and Paul Conrad testifying. Once Kevin recovered from his gunshot wound and his lawyers were ready, his trial would be scheduled on the court docket. There were mixed reviews about Kevin Reed, but most people seemed sympathetic to his role in the abduction, realizing that he was naïve and gullible. He, too, had been deceived by his father, but there had to be some consequences for his actions. They couldn't just be condoned or totally forgiven. There were teachable lessons for Kevin but also society's youth if they were paying attention to this case.

The real victims left in this wake were the Conrad family, Susan and Tommy Stanwick, and, of course, Ramona Reed. Susan Stanwick, Ramona Reed, and Doug Conrad were constantly hounded by reporters, exacerbating the pain they were already enduring. All had suffered tremendous loss. There were no winners in all of this. None.

CHAPTER 97

Nights were the worst for Doug. Coming home to an empty house was unbearable. He tried to purge the thoughts of the married life he once knew, but Cynthia's signature was on everything in the house. He could hear her warm and tender voice speaking to him, her laughter. He wasn't used to not being greeted by her welcoming home kiss. He still hadn't had time to adjust to the change. He couldn't stand to hear the word "*widower*."

There were a few bright spots in Doug's life. Mitch had just been released from the hospital and was sent home to recover. Elaine had been released several days after entering the hospital. Doug had not missed a day visiting her. Elaine was almost fully recovered and could care for Mitch. Doug planned to be there for both of them for as long as they needed him.

Mitch had followed this case via the evening news from his hospital room each day. Doug visited him almost everyday with the exception of the funeral days and provided him with updates. From the night of their attack, Doug had not played an active role in the case and had been actually shut out of the investigation at that point. He was learning his facts from the newscast each day also. He and Mitch would then discuss those facts . These two men had been close before all of this happened, but they were bonded in a way now that they never had been before. Doug felt like he owed Mitch and Elaine everything for protecting his children and putting their very lives in jeopardy to do so. How could he repay them? He couldn't. They bore all of the scars. That is, visible scars. His scars weren't visible, but they would hurt longer than those of the Neubauers, but that wasn't to take anything away from them.

Mitch was getting itchy to get back to work, but it would still be awhile. He, too, would have to testify in court about the night of their attack. So would Elaine. But, then, so would Paul and Taylor. He dreaded that, but he was anxious to see Quinton put away forever. It was going to be a smorgasbord for the local reporters as this drama played out in court. Again, there would be no winners.

Doug let Snuggles out in the backyard to do her thing before bedtime, and then they both climbed the stairs to the bedroom where it all began. Doug pulled the covers down so that Snuggles could jump in the bed and stretch out on Cynthia's pillow. She was so predictable and such a creature of habit. He went into the bathroom and took a long, hot shower. Feeling relaxed but melancholy, he walked over to their Bose stereo and hit Play. Oftentimes he and Cynthia would play a romantic CD and dance in the dark with the moonlight shining in their room. He looked out the window at a beautiful full moon as he waited for the CD to begin playing, not sure really which one was put in last.

He heard Neil Diamond singing . . .

> *"The story of my life is very plain to read,*
> *It starts the day you came*
> *And ends the day you leave . . .*
> *You're the story of my life, and every word is true*
> *Each chapter sings your name*
> *Each page begins with you . . .*
> *The story of my life is very plain to read*
> *It starts the day you came*
> *It ends the day you leave."*

Tears streamed down Doug's face, overwhelmed by memories.

> *"Oh Cynthia . . . my beloved Cynthia . . ."*